THE ATHLETE-STUDENT:
Sophomore Year

Eugene D. Holloman

The Athlete-Student: Sophomore Year

This is a work of fiction. Names, places, characters and incidents either are the product of the author's imagination or are used fictitiously, and any resemblance to actual persons, living or dead businesses, companies, events or locales is entirely coincidental.

ISBN-13: 978-0-578-61495-3

www.theathletestudent.com

Author Email: contact@theathletestudent.com

Editor: Tandylyn Terry
Interior Design: Lauren Michelle
Cover: Marcus Duenas

Contents

Contents

THE ATHLETE-STUDENT:

Sophomore Year

1

Two Thousand Miles Away

"TOOTIE. TOOTIE, GET UP OUT the bed!" my dad screamed from the living room. "Come in here. The game is about to come on."

I yelled back. "Record it for me. I'll watch it later."

Dad burst through my bedroom door like an FBI agent and said, "No, you need to get up out this room. It smells like you haven't showered in days." I started to pull the covers back over my head, dreading the thought of leaving. But, as soon as the blanket reached my forehead, he screamed, "I'm not gonna ask you no more. Get your butt up, NOW! You've been hiding in this room for weeks."

Two weeks to be exact. Ever since the incident happened back in Georgia, I've felt like my life was of little value. I couldn't sleep or eat. And showering? The thought alone was too much to handle. Since being back in Virginia, I've spent most of my time lying in bed, dreaming of being with my teammates. I couldn't explain my emotions, but I thought I didn't have much to live for. With every passing thought and second of the day, I felt like I was going through hell.

Each thought fixated on what had transpired since the media got word of my ineligibility. First, I called my dad to tell him the bad news. It was the toughest phone call I've ever had to make.

When Dad picked up, I asked, "Are you sitting down? I have something to tell you." Because of the tone in my voice, he knew right away — it was about to be bad. "I was ruled ineligible because of my grades. I can't play in the playoff game."

"WHAT?" he asked.

"It's a long story, Dad. I can't travel with the team or practice until further notice. Can you pick me up tomorrow? We're on winter break, and I have to be out of my dorm."

"So, you want me to hop on the road and drive eight hours, huh?" His voice elevated the more he spoke. "You got yourself into this mess, so get yourself out. Find your own ride home."

I didn't know if he was more upset about the embarrassment I caused our family or canceling his flight and hotel out west. Either way, it was only the beginning of the tough conversations. That same day, Coach Stuart made me address the team.

Addressing the team seemed pointless. Everyone in the state had heard what happened. I was sure my teammates knew every detail and had formed their own opinions of the situation by now. It wasn't like I was delivering some breaking news. Coach Stuart just wanted to shame me in front of everybody. He wanted to use me to send a message to my teammates: don't be like Tootie.

As I walked into the team meeting, I still had no idea what I was going to say besides sorry for letting them down. When I entered, everyone's eyes locked directly on me. I swear their stares came with scorching heat. I immediately started to sweat. My throat was desert dry, and I couldn't look anyone directly in their eyes. I focused on the back wall as I stood facing the team while they remained sitting.

"You guys are my brothers and, I mean, I mean, I don't know how ...," I stammered before my throat locked up. No more words came out, but a small flood of tears filled my eyes.

Terrell stood up, wrapped his arms around me, and said, "I forgive you. Use this to make you a better version of yourself."

Afterward, each guy came up and hugged me. I never did get out a formal apology, but through my tears, I was sure they understood I was sorry.

Finally, there was the internet. I'd been threatened and mocked on every college football site known to man. Two weeks ago, they loved me. It was, "Tootie for Heisman." They considered me the best freshman running back since Tony Dorsett. I was showcased on the front pages of sports sections across the country, and now they wanted to kill me. I read one Tweet that said, "University of Georgia's Tootie Mayberry is just like every other thug who only cares about sports." They say you gotta take the good with the bad, but it was hard when they were out there assassinating my character. The love you receive from football is conditional. They love you based on your on-the-field performance. As soon as you stop producing SportsCenter Top 10 plays, the love vanishes.

Have you ever had a day that you wished you could skip in its entirety? Today was that day for me. I was sure it'd be as bad as pulling teeth. I couldn't face it, nor did I want to see what was about to appear on live television. My guys — the men I called brothers — were minutes away from going to battle, thousands of miles away in Pasadena, California, without me. So, can you blame me for dreading this day? For the past two weeks, I laid in bed, wishing this day would magically disappear. But it was here now, and even my dad wouldn't let me run away from it.

When I walked into the living room, I saw Terrell and Keith standing midfield for the National Anthem. As the camera zoomed in, I saw the ferocity in their eyes. There they were, standing in the middle of the Rose Bowl, a place where legends were made. Watching them stand there made me feel my first genuine piece of happiness in weeks. But, when the view changed to our sideline, rage instantly took over my body. I'd spent the last seven months with those guys preparing for that exact moment. Not being there boiled my blood.

"Dang, Tootie, we would've been in the Cali sunshine right now," Shawn said with a grin.

"Say one more thing out your mouth," I responded with anger. "When I punch you, I bet you won't say another word."

"Both of y'all shut up," Dad chimed in.

It didn't take long for the play-by-play announcer to mention my name. "You have to wonder how this Georgia football team is going to respond after losing their sensational freshman running back, Tootie Mayberry, who was recently ruled academically ineligible."

The other announcer chimed in, "Yeah, they're without over 1,400 yards of production. The pressure falls squarely on the shoulders of Terrell Knight, now."

I was in a lose-lose situation. If we lost, I'd be blamed. I could hear the pundits now: "Tootie's immaturity lost Georgia the game before it started. Having to play in the biggest game of the year without one of the players who got you there is a difficult obstacle to overcome." But, if we won, they'd say, "The team does not need a distraction like Tootie. They can win without him."

As the game got underway, I watched each play intensely and intently. My adrenaline was pumping. It was like I was inside the television screen experiencing each moment with my guys. When Marcus almost made an acrobatic interception in the first quarter, it felt like I was right there. I could picture him telling the quarterback from Penn State, "Try me again. I bet I won't drop the next one." I could visualize Terrell saying, "My bad" after a missed throw or rallying the offensive line by encouraging them to keep fighting. As my emotions went in every which direction like a roller coaster, I again felt like a part of the team. I wanted this win just as bad as them.

The game went back and forth through two quarters and was all tied up at 21 at the half. Although our running game was close to non-existent, it was Terrell's arm that kept us one half away from winning. He was digging deep in his bag, doing everything the team needed. When a receiver was open, he found him. When the play broke down, he used his legs. To sum up his first-half performance, the play-by-play announcer used the word "gutsy." Terrell was the best player on the field thus far.

I texted, "Leave it all on the field" followed by a fist pump emoji to Terrell. I didn't know if he'd see it, but I received a message saying, "I got you bro" a minute later. His response made me confident. I knew he was about to give it all he had for the next 30 minutes. Without a doubt, he was going to will this team to victory.

The second half turned out to be a defensive battle. Neither team's offense was able to duplicate the first-half success. We'd move the ball for a little then get stopped and have to punt it away, and their offense did the same.

"Dang, Tootie, I'm not trying to be funny or nothing, but if you were out there, we'd be up two touchdowns," said Shawn.

Giving him a side-eye, I nodded my head and refocused on the television screen. But deep down, I knew Shawn was right. The world knew he was right. Penn State made second-half adjustments, knocking Terrell out of his game. Not posing a threat on the ground made it easier for them to lock in on his strengths. The first and second half were day and night by comparison. In the second half, we couldn't get in a good offensive rhythm.

This game was going to come down to the wire. The team that made a game-changing play to shift momentum in their favor would be victorious. I'd literally have given my right hand to be in that situation. Millions of people were watching around the world, and there was an opportunity to become a national hero. I dreamed of this moment my whole life. I wanted to be there as bad as I could breathe. I couldn't sit and watch any longer. I stood up, went outside, and paced back and forth in our driveway.

Several minutes later, after getting my anxiety into check, I went back inside. Penn State had gone up by seven points with only a minute and a half to play.

"Dang, how'd they score so fast?" I asked Dad and Shawn.

"Your boy Marcus got torched on a double move down the sideline," Shawn answered. "You might wanna call him after the game."

And just like that, the ball and game were in Terrell's hands. I bet he wouldn't have wanted it any other way. This was one more chance to show NFL scouts why he was the best college quarterback in the world and a first-round draft pick.

Like a well-oiled machine, Terrell led the offense on a drive that had a recipe for greatness. Calmly, he started it with a quick strike for eight yards before hurrying the team to the line for the next play. Then, he flawlessly reeled off a missile down the middle of the field between two defenders for another 20 yards.

With only the clock working against us, Terrell orchestrated three more successful plays. We were within 10 yards of evening the score and going into overtime. Twenty seconds remained, more than enough time to score.

I could feel my nerves building up with the next play. Instead of going outside again, I turned my head away from the television and listened as the announcer said, "It's a three-receiver set with one running back and one tight end. Terrell Knight drops back, pumps fake to the right, spins out to his left to avoid a sack, and throws a laser to the back pylon............. IT'S INTERCEPTED, IT'S INTERCEPTED! That should do it, ladies and gentlemen, that should do it. What a costly throw by Georgia's Terrell Knight. You have to think he wishes he had that throw back. Why didn't he throw the ball out of bounds instead of forcing it? It's a throw the whole state of Georgia wish they could have back."

As I turned my head around to watch the television, the camera quickly showed a distraught Terrell before turning to our fans. They either had their jaws on the floor or hands over their heads in disbelief.

In total shock, I immediately dropped to the floor in a fetal position.

2

WHERE DO I GO FROM HERE?

"IT'S JUST A GAME, TOOTIE." That's what Sophia would tell me after a loss in high school. It wasn't what she said after those tough defeats, it was how she said it. She'd pull me in close, wrap her arms around me tightly as the fragrance she wore made the hairs on the back of my neck rise, and look deeply into my eyes, while speaking with the gentlest tone imaginable.

It had been a week since the heart-wrenching defeat to Penn State. All Shawn and Dad did was walk around the house like the game never happened. Not once did I get, "How are you feeling?" or "If you wanna talk about it, I'm here."

They pressed the off button on the television remote and didn't think about that game ever again. And to some extent I got it. Although they had followed the team all year, they didn't have an emotional connection to it as strong as I did. They had no idea what it was like to eat, sleep, and breathe football for months then lose a game in the last seconds. Not to mention, doing all of that and being suspended for the biggest game of the year. But my relationship with Sophia was so close that she could feel my emotions. She knew what to say and do at the right time. Her comforting words were the only medicine I needed to heal from those tough losses.

I hadn't talked to Sophia since we broke up over three months ago. While I tried texting her a time or two, I never received a response, and rightfully so. I threw four and a half years down the drain for a lousy two minutes of pleasure. What hurt the most was knowing that she'd heard about my ineligibility by now and never thought to check if I was okay. She couldn't hate me that much. Then again, maybe she could. I bet she watched the game on the television and enjoyed every minute of me not being there with the team. She probably smirked when the announcer talked about how much I put the team's chances in jeopardy.

I knew she was home on winter break from James Madison University. So, I texted her saying, "I'm back home if you didn't already know. It'd be nice to see you over the break to catch up. No pressure or anything but I've been thinking about you and would like to see you."

She received my message immediately but didn't respond until almost 30 minutes later. It said, "It's good to hear from you. I'm pretty busy for the next week, or so but afterward, we can go out for lunch or something."

"That'd be nice," I replied. I left the conversation there. I didn't want to push it too far or sound desperate.

Later that night, the National Championship game was set to come on. Penn State versus the University of Oklahoma. I told myself I wasn't going to trip about it. In fact, I wasn't going to watch it. Why put extra stress on me? All I'd do was think about my mistakes and pummel myself further into the ground by repeating, "We should be playing right now."

I knew Dad would have the game blasting through the living room speakers, so I asked Shawn, "Do you wanna see a movie tonight?"

"Man, how would I look sitting next to another grown man in a movie theater?" he responded.

"It's not like we're going to see a romance flick."

"Man, I was just joking. What time are you tryna go?"

"Around 8:30."

"Ohhhhhh. You think pops will make you watch the game tonight, huh?"

"You know how he is. He won't say a word the whole time the game is on but expect us to sit there and watch it with him."

Later that night, Shawn and I escaped Dad's invitation to watch the game and went to see an action movie.

After buying our tickets, we found the perfect seats. I was just getting settled when Shawn looked over, right after the movie previews started, and whispered, "Go get some popcorn. Oh, and make sure it has extra butter on it."

"Nah man, you go get some. You know I like seeing what's about to come out."

"I paid for your ticket after you asked me to come."

Shawn got me there. So, I reluctantly got up and went to the concession stand. After ordering a big tub of popcorn with extra butter and an extra pinch of salt, I saw a young lady with a short and slim stature standing with her back toward me. Even with her back turned, I still noticed her caramel complexion and short black hair. For a second, I thought it was Sophia, but her hair wasn't that short. Sophia's hair was down to her lower back.

Nah, that couldn't be her, I said to myself. I walked in her direction as discreetly as I could. When I got closer, I dropped my tub of popcorn out of complete shock. I didn't drop it because I confirmed it was Sophia. I dropped it because she was with another guy.

"Hey, Sophia," I greeted. "I almost didn't recognize you with your new haircut. I like it."

"Oh, heeeeeeey Tootie," she said, sounding as if she was surprised to see me.

"Hey, what's up, man?" I asked the guy she was on a date with.

"Tootie, this is Corey. Corey, this is Tootie," Sophia interrupted.

17

"I see you moved on quickly," I said sarcastically.

"This is not the time or place," she responded.

"So, the time and place is a couple of weeks from now when we go to lunch, huh?" I asked.

"My man, chill," Corey chimed in. "You starting to make a scene."

Corey stood no taller than 5'9 and didn't weigh any more than 170 pounds. Not saying it meant much but I could probably drag him across the movie theater if I wanted. At that point, I was agitated. If he said one more thing out of pocket, he was all mine. But before I let it get to that point, I calmly said to Corey, "With all due respect, this ain't got nothing to do with you."

"What do you mean? You were talking to my lady, homie. It definitely has something to do with me Toot," Corey retorted.

"Toot? Come on man, you disrespecting me right now," I said. "And what do you mean by 'my lady'?"

Sophia didn't flinch when I asked about their relationship. Moving closer to her, I grabbed her hand, looked directly into her eyes, and asked, "So, what's this? If you moved on, I'll ...."

Before I could get out what I was trying to say, Corey slapped my wrist away from Sophia's hand

and shoved me backward. Corey didn't know I was waiting for him to touch me. He also didn't realize I had so much anger within me from everything that had happened in the last few months. He became the perfect person to release my wrath on.

Without hesitation, I staggered my left foot in front of the right one and cocked my right hand back and drove it right into Corey's nose. I was just about to follow up with a left punch, but the first one did the trick. I hit Corey so hard that he fell into an old arcade race car seat.

Before I could turn around and finish what I was saying to Sophia, Shawn came out of nowhere and dragged me out of the movie theater. He didn't let go of me until we got back to his car.

Out of breath, Shawn looked over at me from the driver seat as he drove away and said, "Why you knock that boy out like that?"

"He put his hands on me. Then I just blacked out."

"Man, you trippin' Tootie. You know I spent time behind bars for knocking somebody out like you just did."

"Shawn, you used a gun. I used my fist."

"Do you think the police care if a weapon or your fist was used?"

All of a sudden it hit me. I could get into some serious trouble. That right-hand jab could cost me everything. Although it felt good, I started to get sick to my stomach. I just knew the cops would be at the house waiting for me.

"You think anybody saw it, Shawn?" I asked once we arrived in front of our home.

"What kinda dumb question is that? How do you think I knew to come out there?"

"Man, it's probably on the internet by now."

"I wouldn't be surprised."

"Dang, I keep on doing stupid stuff."

"I saw Sophia standing there. I know you weren't fighting over her, bro."

"I don't know what I was fighting over, to be honest."

Shawn chuckled. "Man, all I saw was that boy feet in the air. I guess I at least taught you something."

"You always gotta throw a joke in there, huh?"

"It wouldn't be me if I didn't. Well, let's go in this house. Do you wanna tell Dad, or should I?" Shawn asked.

"Why do we need to tell him for?"

"It's better to tell him before he finds out about it from somewhere else."

The Penn State and Oklahoma game was still on when we walked into the house. Penn State was up by a wide margin. They had the National Championship in the bag. I assumed Dad had lost interest with the score being out of reach and all, so I sat on the couch beside him and told him what had happened less than an hour ago.

As expected, my dad's first reaction was the same as a brick wall. He sat on the couch, stiff and unemotional for about two minutes until he gathered his thoughts.

Finally, he looked over at me while shaking his head and said, "You don't get it?" Rubbing his temple, he resumed, "You just don't get it, do you?"

"I do get it, Dad," I replied.

"You obviously don't. Let me explain something to you."

I nodded my head to show I was attentive and eager to hear what he had to say.

"When you have a dream, and everything seems to be headed in the right direction, life will throw you subtle obstacles to see how you'll react. Those obstacles are designed to knock you off course, designed to see how bad you want it. You were on top of the world a few months ago, and then boom, little bumps in the road were thrown at you. They were small bumps, but since you were unfocused, they seemed massive. First, it was not taking an hour or two to study so that you could be on top of your coursework. Small, right?"

"Yes," I mumbled.

"But it turned out to be huge. Name splattered in the media for simply not taking two hours out your day. Now it's this. You have a chance to get everything back on track. But no, you decide to punch someone in public like people don't know who you are. You let 10 seconds of anger potentially cost you your freedom. Hey, but you know it all, Tootie. You have to live with your consequences, not me. One thing I don't do is jail. I promise if you go, I will not be there."

3

Georgia on Our Minds

AFTER THE MOVIE THEATER INCIDENT, I was more paranoid than a person being chased by a chainsaw-carrying villain in a scary movie. Each day I anticipated a police officer coming to arrest me. The thought of being placed in a cop car with handcuffs cutting off the circulation in my wrists made me duck and hide every time I heard a police siren. You would've thought I was on America's Most Wanted list. Besides being terrified of getting arrested, I regularly checked the internet to see if any videos surfaced of me knocking out Sophia's new man, Corey. I drew a blank when replaying the incident in my head. It could've been 100 or 200 people around.

The details from that night were fuzzy. I didn't remember much of anything after Shawn pulled me away. One thing I did know was that the University of Georgia would ship me out of town as fast as lightning if I got arrested or a video popped up.

I only had a couple of days left before I had to head back to Georgia to start the spring semester. I thought I was in the clear until I received a phone call from Coach Perkins.

"I heard about … Hold up let me rephrase that, I saw your Mike Tyson impersonation on video," he said.

"What?" I blurted out after hearing him loud and clear.

"One of my students who was at the movies recorded the whole thing."

"Are you serious?" I asked.

"He told me he has no interest in shaming you and to the best of his knowledge, no one else has a recording of the incident. All he wants you to do is come and sign some apparel, and the video will be long gone."

"You sure he hasn't sent it to anyone else?" I questioned. "How do I know he won't try and post it at a later date?"

"Trust me. I can vouch for this kid."

"You haven't reached out this entire time I been in Georgia, and now you want me to trust you?"

"Come on, Tootie. I always had your best interest at heart. I knew you were upset with me about the whole University of Virginia thing, so I stayed away. I was only trying to push you in that direction because I knew for sure they'd treat you like family. I had no hidden agenda whatsoever. For what it's worth, I kept tabs on you through your father."

"I hear you Coach P, but my father didn't play for you for four years either," I responded. "Anyway, I need that video gone as soon as possible."

"Just come into my office, and it'll be done. You also have to do me a favor, too."

"What's that, Coach?"

"Come and talk to the football team. Be candid with them about your experiences thus far. I think the things you've been through in such a short amount of time would be impactful."

"I don't know, Coach. I mean, I don't know if I'm ready for all of that yet."

"Some of the things we go through are not just for us. Others need to hear them. So, whenever you are ready, just let me know."

I rushed over to my old high school to see Coach P that same afternoon. When I walked into the gymnasium, the entire football team was there working out in the adjacent weight room. I avoided being noticed and slipped into Coach P's office. Upon entering, there was Coach and a skinny little kid named Ben, who looked as innocent as a ladybug.

I introduced myself and expressed gratitude for the way the whole video ordeal was handled. Encountering a kid like this one was rare. As far as I could tell, there were no ulterior motives. Ben only wanted a couple of University of Georgia hats and t-shirts signed. Little did he know, I'd sign his forehead if it meant this incident would be behind me.

After signing the items and taking a picture with Ben, he stepped back and said, "By the way, I was never going to post or send the video to anyone. I saw the guy touch you first. If anyone had seen the video, they'd miss the part where you remained calm and were provoked. They would've only seen the punch and deemed you a villain. In my eyes, you're a legend around here, and I don't want your story to end like that."

After several more minutes of talking with Ben, I learned he became a huge fan after entering high school last year. He mentioned how scared he was to speak to me when he saw me around school. Ben thought I was this unapproachable, big man on campus my senior year, which was his freshman year. For the first time, I had to ask myself if I fit the narrative of being another egotistical athlete. *How did I not embrace Ben and the younger kids in my school and community?* I'd made everything about me, and that was evident from our conversation.

After Ben left the office, I looked at Coach P and asked, "What was it like around here after word got out about my ineligibility?"

Coach took a deep breath and exhaled before saying, "It was devastating. Everyone was hurt because the media portrayed you to be something that you're not. I do know everyone's rooting for you. We all wanna see you get back on track. I want you to do well in school and get your degree."

"Yes sir," I responded.

"Do you know the requirements for getting your eligibility back?" Coach P asked.

"I have no idea. I'll find out when I head back for the spring semester."

"Tootie, I don't wanna give you any long lectures because I've given you plenty over the years. But son, you have to take school more seriously. If you don't, you'll live with constant regret when your football career is over," said Coach P.

With firm eye contact, I replied, "You're right. I finally see what you been preaching all these years. It was a tough lesson to learn, but I finally got it. I only wish I would've listened instead of going through it first-hand, you know?"

"I know, Tootie. I'm thrilled it's resonating with you, son."

"Coach, if you don't mind, I'd like to take you up on your offer to talk to the team. I'm ready after all."

There were only a handful of players remaining from the squad I played on, but each player dapped me up as if they knew me for years. The respect and admiration they showed allowed me to relax before addressing them.

Without any hesitation, I began by saying, "Every time I've ever taken a shortcut, or what I thought would be the easiest route, I've always had to start over further back than where I began. I decided to cheat on an exam, and that's the reason I couldn't play in the College Football Playoff game. It not only cost me, it cost my teammates and our university a chance at winning a national championship. I went from being loved to hated, faster than a New York minute. Now I have to go back to school and start all over. I have to rebuild my reputation from the ground up. I'll probably have some teammates who'll never wanna talk to me again. All because I took the easy route instead of putting in the work. So, my thing to you guys is, you cannot cheat the grind. Whether it's football or a math test, you'll get out what you put in. It's as simple as that."

After speaking for a few more minutes, I opened the floor for questions. I immediately thought I'd put my foot in my mouth as every hand raised. They probably wanted to know all about my suspension or gain clarity on some of the rumors they heard.

The first player I pointed to was a fellow running back, and he asked, "What advice would you give me as I one day hope to play big-time college ball like you?"

I thought for a moment, and then replied, "I didn't realize how important your ninth- and tenth-grade years were. Those years play an important part in your grade point average. So, my advice to you would be to take school seriously now rather than trying to play catch up your senior year. It'll save you from many headaches when trying to get a certain SAT score."

That was a good question, but it was a warm-up. The next question I received was, "What's it like trying to handle sports and schoolwork in college?"

"Not trying to scare you guys or anything, but it's like having two full-time jobs. Most jobs you work for eight hours a day and then go home. But in college, you work 16 to 18 hours a day. Your day might start at 5 a.m., and you won't be done until 11 p.m."

The last question I got was the hardest. I was asked, "Do you have any regrets?"

"A lot of people will sit here and lie and say something cliché. They'd say something like, 'I would do the same thing over again because it made me who I am'. But for me, I'd change a lot. I made some bad decisions, and as you guys know, it cost me. So yes, I have regrets. The hardest thing for me is living with my regrets knowing I could've avoided most things in the first place."

I left shortly after their questions, so I wasn't too sure of the impact my little speech had on the guys. But I know it freed me from months of agony. I had so much weighing me down, but afterward, it felt like the chains that were around my ankles were starting to disappear. I knew I had some mountains to climb when I got back to Georgia, but I was ready for whatever I had to do.

• • •

Heading to Athens, Georgia, was much different than it was when I first made the trip over seven months ago. The eight-hour drive seemed like 20 hours this time around. Dad drove again while Shawn rode in the front seat. But this time, there was no excitement. There was no joy. No music. No talking. The journey was filled with anxious expectations of facing whatever we were going to see once we arrived.

Shawn broke the awkward silence and said, "This car ride is just like the bus ride I took to prison. It had to be at least 40 other prisoners on that bus with me. Nobody said a word the entire four-hour drive. All we could think about was what was going to happen once we got there. So, if y'all don't want me having flashbacks, somebody needs to either start a conversation, turn on the radio, or something. Geesh!"

Well, I was glad jail wasn't on the other end of the drive. But still, I didn't know what to expect once we got there. I anticipated my arrival to be like Shawn's arrival at prison. Just as the other inmates taunted the new prisoners with name-calling, howling, and threats, I expected the student body to do the same. I received plenty at opposing stadiums and rightfully so. But the thought of getting the same treatment from my own hurt a bit.

Pulling up to my dorm sent shock waves through my body. Being back on campus for the first time since all of that happened was the scariest feeling I'd ever felt. No more hiding and running from my mistakes. I couldn't lay in bed all day and not face the world as I did for most of the winter break back in Virginia. And as short as it may have seemed, the walk I was about to make to my dorm was daunting. It was the first step in my redemption process.

Alright, here we go. I took a deep breath before getting out of the car. I could feel the students who were outside staring at me. If their looks could kill, I would've dropped dead. After walking for a minute, I was cool with the stares. They didn't bother me too much, but I worried about the verbal assaults most. Upon reaching the elevator within the residence hall, no one had said a word to me.

All that changed as I waited with Dad and Shawn for the elevator to come back down. I could feel this kid, who was waiting for it too, watching me like a hawk. I tried my hardest to ignore his beaming stares, but it was too blatant to overlook.

"What's up, man?" I asked as we all stepped onto the elevator.

"Aren't you Tootie?" he responded.

"Yeah, that's me," I answered while simultaneously pushing the elevator button to go to the third floor.

"You not playing in the playoff game was tough luck for the both of us. I lost $500 on that game," he said.

I didn't say a word, just gave him a head nod. But he kept talking. "Hit those books harder next time. That's what we're here for anyway. Well, maybe not you but for the rest of the students."

"What do you mean by that?" I snapped.

"What do you think I meant?" the student sneered.

"Man, what's your major?" I demanded.

"Education."

"We'll see who's laughing when I'm making millions in the NFL in a few years while you're struggling to find a school to teach at."

With a grin, he taunted, "You'll be lucky to make it to your sophomore year."

I almost lost it. But, luckily for him, the elevator reached my floor. I surely wasn't about to let him play me like that. He didn't know my story or what I'd been through. I knew the talking was gonna come, but I couldn't let people say anything to me and get away with it.

"Son, you have to remember the heckling comes with it," my dad said as we walked off the elevator toward my dorm room.

"I know, I know," I grumbled, while flashing back momentarily to the still fresh movie theater incident.

"The moment you lose your cool will be the moment you throw everything away. That's what people want you to do. I didn't say anything on the elevator because I wanted to see how you were going to handle it. Trust me, if you continue to go back and forth with every agitator, they'll eventually get to you. It only takes one time for you to snap, just one time and you'll lose everything you've worked for," Dad said.

"Dude, you look like somebody stole your bike," Marcus mocked after we walked into the dorm room.

I responded, "I'm good man."

"Marcus, do me a favor and keep an eye out for Tootie," said Dad.

"Dad, I'm good. You don't have to ask anyone to watch me," I interrupted.

After Dad and Shawn left, I told Marcus to look out for me. Dad was right. I was just too stubborn to admit it. This semester would make or break me, and I'd be a fool to think I could handle everything that'd be thrown my way by myself.

4

Right of Redemption

I DON'T REMEMBER THE EXACT quote, but my favorite rapper, Tupac, once said something like, "Through every dark night, there is a brighter day. So, no matter how hard life gets, keep your chin up and handle it." I reflected on his words as I woke up the next morning with only two things on my agenda. Up first was a visit to my academic advisor, Mr. Hernandez. Whatever he said I had to do to regain my eligibility, then that was what I'd do. Even if I had to spend the entire spring semester studying for six hours a night and not go to a single party, then so be it. After visiting Mr. Hernandez, I had to see what my coaches were talking about. I wasn't sure if they were over the playoff loss yet. They were either still holding a grudge against me or looking forward to spring ball and our upcoming season. Either way, I was prepared for whatever they were going to throw my way.

When I walked into Mr. Hernandez's office, he said, "Shut the door behind you." Shutting his door meant he was about to have a man-to-man conversation that wasn't meant for anyone else's ears.

"Welcome back. I'm sure you had an emotional winter break, huh, Tootie?"

Instead of verbally answering, I gave a quick head nod.

"Well, we're here now. What has transpired, can't be changed. But, you can remember the feelings from it all and do everything within your power to ensure nothing like this happens again," Mr. Hernandez added.

"Yes sir! That's the only way to go about it," I replied while exhaling deeply.

"I thought about you a lot during the break and especially during the playoff game." His voice picked up. "I'm extremely proud of you."

"What is there to be proud of?" I asked confused.

"Most kids who go through what you're going through will run and hide. They'd look to transfer and start fresh elsewhere. From what I can tell, you're looking forward to facing your problems head-on."

"I mean, I let everyone down. Including myself. There's nothing I can do besides stick it out and correct my wrongs."

Mr. Hernandez declared, "You know what, Tootie, let me tell you something that most academic advisors who want to keep their job wouldn't say."

"What's that?"

"This stays between you and me. We, as in the administration, failed you."

"What makes you say that?"

"Because we know public perception is an important thing in our society. Do you understand what I mean when I say public perception?" Mr. Hernandez asked.

"Yes! It's what everybody thinks about you."

"You're right. And while we recognize an 18-year-old made a huge mistake, we still allowed the media to tarnish your name. Everywhere I turned people were bashing you. Nobody from this university has said much on your behalf. The reason why, even though nobody will admit it, was because you essentially cost the school millions of dollars by not winning a national championship. Whether you like it or not, you're the scapegoat. So, everything you do from here on out will be under a microscope. Truth be told, this is a critical semester for you."

What Mr. Hernandez was saying was a lot to take in. I tried to think of a fitting response, but I had nothing. I settled for a shoulder shrug while simultaneously shaking my head.

He must've read my mind because he went on to say, "I know this is a lot to absorb but I have to keep it as real as I can."

"I appreciate that. I mean, I thought about what I cost the university but, in my mind, it's just a game. It never resonated with me that millions were at stake," I stated.

"Yeah, Tootie! You have to recognize the school is gonna get what they need out of you. So, you have to get something out of this, too. Getting drafted in the first round would be great, but it's too early to tell if that's gonna happen. So, the next best thing is to make sure you're taking advantage of your education."

"Yes sir, Mr. Hernandez. I'm going to stay on top of things this semester."

"I registered you for 16 credit hours. It may seem like a lot but as you know, you have much more time on your hands this spring compared to the fall. With that said, you have to use your time wisely. The goal is to maintain a 3.0 grade point average. You got this, Tootie."

That went better than I imagined, I said to myself as I left Mr. Hernandez's office. The only way that morning would've been better was if I could say the same thing after meeting with the coaches. From experience, I learned two things about our coaching staff.

First, there was nothing better than hanging around the coaches the week after winning a game in which you played well. For the entire week, their offices would turn into the hangout spot for the players. They'd fill the lobby with all types of cookies, doughnuts, candy, and other delicacies for us to grab. The relaxed atmosphere included coaches engaging in conversation while even telling occasional jokes here and there. If I could sum up the mood in the office the week after a win, it would be equal to walking in your sweet grand mamma's home and smelling your favorite dish being prepared just for you.

Second, anything and everything was better than being around the coaches after losing a game. Hanging around their offices that week, you'd be lucky to get a "Hi" from one of them. If you absolutely had to go into the office, you might be the only player around. Everyone stayed away. Just like a desert, the offices were a dark, lonesome place that nobody wanted to visit.

So, my approach before meeting with the coaches was to mentally prepare as if we just lost a game the week before. I braced myself to walk into an environment that sucked the joy from your body as soon as you stepped inside. I was convinced there wasn't going to be any warm welcomes. As far as I knew, I was the enemy headed into uncharted territory.

"Tootie, come into my office for a second and shut the door behind you," said my running back coach, Coach White, as he spotted me entering the football facility. Ironically, he wanted his door shut just like Mr. Hernandez, so you know how I thought our conversation was about to go.

Before Coach White could state his disappointment and tell me what was needed to regain some trust, I decided to get in front of it by saying, "Coach, I know I hurt this team. I know everyone is probably still mad for what I put them through. I'm gonna do everything in my power to fix what I broke."

"Look, Tootie, for this team to get where we think we can go, we have to move on. I'm moving on and I hope you do as well. You're a key piece of this team and my job is to help you going forward. But for me to do that, you have to be honest with me. It's hard to read you and if you don't open your mouth, I have no idea what you're going through. So, going forward we'll have weekly meetings just –"

Before Coach White could finish his sentence, our head coach knocked at his door. Coach Stuart walked in and patted my back before taking a seat beside me and across from Coach White.

"Sorry for the interruption, Coach. Please continue," a cheerful Coach Stuart said to Coach White.

"Yes sir, Coach," Coach White responded. "Tootie, going forward we'll have weekly meetings just to chat about everything besides football. Everything happened so fast last season. And to be honest, I don't know how I would've handled everything if I was in your shoes. So, I'll be the first to apologize for not leading you correctly. For that I take responsibility."

"Just to echo some of Coach White's sentiments, Tootie, you have a clean slate. Last season is last season. You can participate in all spring activities. But, by the time your sophomore season starts this fall, you must have a 2.0 grade point average. To help with achieving eligibility, you've been assigned a tutor. You must meet with your tutor four days a week. Do what you're supposed to do, and let's go and win a national championship."

During my recruitment process, the coaches said they'd treat me like family, but I was skeptical about it. I mean, all coaches say that. But family forgives and moves on. That's what they were doing with me and I was appreciative of it all. They could've exiled me out of there but instead, they gave me a second chance. Their willingness to move on and allow me to start fresh, freed me from all my anxiety. Over the past year, every time I made a mistake, I suffered the consequences. Sophia caught me cheating and dumped me. I cheated on a test and got suspended. This was the first time in a long time where I felt I'd been given a second chance. I knew I had to take this opportunity seriously.

My mind was on cloud nine as I left the coaches' office to officially start my spring semester. I placed headphones over my ears and cranked up the volume to some classic Bob Marley before walking to my Geography of Human Rights class. Positive vibes were the only thing I welcomed. If anyone said something slick out of their mouths, the sounds of the late, great Jamaican legend would drown it out.

After arriving to class, I sat in the front row and took notes on everything the professor said. I could tell the Geography of Human Rights course was going to take hours of studying. One requirement was looking into national policies and addressing violations, which would require a lot of reading and memorizing. But still, I was up for the challenge.

I kept the momentum of starting on the right foot in my next course, too. The only difference was this course was a repeat from the one I failed in the fall. After class, I went up to Professor Roberts and apologized again for the whole cheating thing. He let me know that he received just as much flack as I did. I didn't realize the scrutiny a teacher could face for failing a star player. He mentioned he thought about leaving the school altogether but decided against it. My decisions were a domino effect. I put Professor Roberts in a tough situation. Other professors and staff that loved the football team were upset with him because of him failing me. I told him I was going to put maximum effort into his class this time around. We shook hands and from what I could tell, there was understanding and mutual respect between us.

After leaving Professor Roberts' class, I headed to lunch with Marcus and a couple of other teammates. As I chowed down on a double cheeseburger and waffle fries, Marcus asked, "Who do you think will take Terrell's spot at quarterback?"

I shrugged my shoulders nonchalantly and chuckled before saying, "It don't even matter. As motivated as I'll be next season, all the new quarterback will have to do is hand me the rock."

"I bet we get a transfer from another school," one of my other teammates chimed in.

Another said, "The freshman, Mitchell Bradley, will shock some people."

"Speaking of transfers, I heard that running back Lamar Barnes from Notre Dame transferred here," Marcus blurted out.

"WHAT?" I shouted. "That's dumb. Why would he transfer here?"

Rumor had it, Lamar, who graduated from Notre Dame, was free to play his last season without having to sit out a year like most transfers were obligated to do. But, I couldn't figure out why he didn't go into the NFL draft. He rushed for over a thousand yards last year. I wasn't worried about competing against him or anything, but I was surprised. I was surprised he chose to go to Georgia knowing I was there. I was also surprised the coaches didn't tell me this news when we met. Maybe, the coaches told Lamar he would start over me. Maybe, all that stuff they said about a clean slate was all a joke. I knew it was too good to be true.

I had one more class, English Composition, then a team meeting. Before lunch, I was dreading our team meeting. It was going to be my first encounter with the entire team since I addressed them all after I was ruled ineligible. All the attention was going to be on me. But after the news I just received, the spotlight would be deflected to our big-time transfer. I couldn't wait to observe our coaches and their reaction to their new best friend Lamar.

I didn't pay not one bit of attention in English Composition. I know I told myself sitting in the front of the class was the new dedicated me, but during class, I sat all the way in the back. I watched the clock the entire time until class let out. Once I got to our team meeting, my only objective was to find and size up Lamar. I wanted to see the guy who was trying to block my comeback story.

As players entered the meeting room, my eyes were glued to the door to see who came in next. And then boom, I located Lamar. He looked human to me. He didn't look as physically imposing as I thought he would. But he certainly didn't look like a scrub either. He stood about 5'11 and roughly 200 pounds. Typical of most running backs at that level.

Coach Stuart addressed the team, and for the most part, it all sounded like gibberish until he called Lamar up to the front to introduce himself. Coach couldn't grab my attention, but Lamar surely did. He looked right in my direction as he spoke. But still, I wasn't certain he was staring at me. Lamar told the team why he chose to leave Notre Dame and go to Georgia.

He said, "I felt like you guys were a running back away from being crowned national champions."

My eyes promptly got as wide as tennis balls. I could feel my teammates peek over at me to see how I was going to react to his subtle jab. I didn't feed into it. Aside from my eyes getting bigger, I tried to hide any other facial expression. Lamar, still glancing in my direction, locked eyes with me. Either he knew who I was already, or my teammates gave it away by looking at me after his national championship remark. One thing was for sure: Lamar's stare officially confirmed a rivalry between the two of us.

He closed his introduction still looking in my direction. "I could've entered into the draft, but I only had one goal before coming to college and it was winning a national championship. So, hopefully, I can help this team achieve it this upcoming season."

5

Spring Breakin'

"TOOTIE, YOUR TUTOR IS FLY," Marcus declared.

"Huh?"

"Man, you heard me. How many classes do I have to fail to get her to tutor me?"

After laughing out loud, I told Marcus, "I don't be checking her out like that. I'm just glad her help got me at a 3.3 grade point average right now. The only time I ever saw a 3.3 was after being clocked in a 40-yard dash."

"Two lies told," Marcus said sarcastically. "Either you still stuck on Sophia or you foolin' yourself. She's way too fine for you not to take notice."

"Alright man. She is fine but I'm too focused right now. We're about to start spring ball and I can't get caught up in all that lovey-dovey stuff."

"There you go still lying to me, bro. I know you man, what's holding you back?"

"Dang Marcus, you're gonna pull it out of me, huh?"

"Sure am!" he barked.

"Man, she's super smart plus she's just as gorgeous as Sophia. In fact, she reminds me of her. I ain't got time for it, bro."

Marcus smirked then tightened up his face before saying, "The old heads back home in South Carolina used to tell me, 'You only get one good girl in your life, and two if you lucky'."

"What? That's some down south wisdom, huh?" I said jokingly.

All jokes aside, I was acing all of my courses thanks to my tutor, Brianna. Seeing her four times a week after a couple of months was a major confidence booster. She had this unexplainable energy about her. Let Marcus tell it, I was more focused around her because of her beauty. But honestly, she simplified assignments better than my professors.

I was freaking out about a huge project I had to present in front of my entire Geography of Human Rights class about the human rights revolution. The scary part was talking about a topic with dates ranging from post-World War II to present times. The instructions my professor gave were vague at best. The instructions read: "Prepare an oral presentation by critically examining the idea of human rights by analyzing a particular space at a particular time. Through your presentation be sure to include what constitutes a human right and a human right violation."

Huh? I hadn't the slightest clue until Brianna explained during one of our tutoring sessions to be creative and speak about something to which I could relate. Then it hit me. I prepared a presentation on the prison system and the treatment of inmates. I relied on some of Shawn's experiences from his time in prison, along with heavy research. I nailed the 15-minute presentation and received two points from a perfect score for my effort.

Brianna deserved most of the credit, but I do believe the spring semester played a vital role in my educational resurgence. For the past two months, there were no games to prepare for. There was no pressure to perform well on Saturdays. There were no hours spent trying to relieve my body from the aches and pains in our training room. There was no studying the playbook or watching film on upcoming opponents for hours. All that occurred since the start of the semester was weight-lifting and conditioning. It was like an extra stress-free six hours were added to my day.

Well, I may have overemphasized the "extra stress-free" part because conditioning was no joke. Every day we pushed our bodies to exhaustion. We did everything from pulling a sled with three-times our body weight up and down the field, running stadium stairs until our legs felt like noodles, to flipping a monster truck tire working muscles we never knew we had.

Some of my teammates complained about the weather being too cold or the excessive number of sprints our strength and conditioning coaches added to workouts. But not me, I embraced the hard workouts. I gave everything I had in each drill. If we had to do 20, 110-yard sprints, I did 30. I made it my goal to outwork the entire team because of what Mr. Hernandez said about perception when we met earlier in the semester. I understood how I was perceived. I was sure people thought I was this lazy and untrustworthy kid. I knew my teammates were watching me like a hawk. They wanted to know if I could be counted on. So, each day I gave everything I had to prove I could be their leader.

I also remembered what it was like when I first arrived in Georgia aiming for Dominque Jones' spot. Lamar was trying his best to compete with me in every drill. In any competition, there's a hidden psychological component. If he thought he was working harder than me, then he'd think he was better and deserved the starting spot. That's what I did with Dominque, so I was far too familiar with Lamar's approach. If he wanted my spot he'd have to take it.

• • •

Before Lamar and I could officially start our must-see competition on the field during spring football activities, there was a much-needed week-long break. Most of the privileged students headed to places like Cancun or the Bahamas. However, the way my bank account was set up, I'd be lucky to get to the other side of town for spring break. I had two options: go back home to Virginia Beach or spend spring break with Marcus in South Carolina. I chose the latter. The last time I was home, I was almost arrested. So, the last thing I wanted to happen was to run into Sophia, the police, or anybody else who'd remind me of the past.

Charleston, South Carolina was everything I envisioned, mostly due to Google & YouTube searches, but still. As soon as we entered Charleston's city lines, I was haunted by some of the things I read on the internet. Visualizing the millions of slaves and stories of racial tension the city endured rattled my brain for a second. But those thoughts didn't last long as I began to notice the box Chevy's everywhere I turned. Just like in the YouTube videos, they were sitting as high as school buses due to the 30-inch chrome rims and tires. It was like they were competing to see who had the best paint jobs and the loudest speakers. Marcus lived in, from what I could tell, a close-knit housing project on the north side of the city. Everybody knew who he was. From senior citizens to toddlers, the clerk at the corner store to the postman — Marcus was a local celebrity.

Every member of our team thought their neighborhood was the toughest in the world. We'd literally spent hours in the locker room debating what made our area the roughest. It was one of those unresolvable debates. Like the Jordan, Kobe, LeBron arguments, it just went on and on. I stayed away from the toughest community debates being from a lower-middle-class area. But after seeing Marcus' housing projects, I'd happily debate on his behalf. Marcus wasn't ashamed either, he was proud of where he came from. Since I'd known him, he talked about getting drafted and moving his mom and son away from the hood. But he didn't want to take them away and forget about the housing projects that had made him. He wanted to give back and be a role model for other kids who lived there. His heart and genuine love for his community were one of the reasons why I wanted to come visit for spring break.

I didn't know it was possible to gain more respect for a person whom you already had the highest appreciation for. But the bond Marcus and his 2-year-old son Marcus Jr. had with each other added another level to the already lofty admiration I had for him. I couldn't manage school, sports, and fatherhood at 19 years old, but Marcus handled it with ease. Not to mention being hours away from home.

"I had an idea of some of the pressure you faced, but I didn't know the extent until now," I said to Marcus. "You have your whole hood, your mother, and your son putting their hope in you."

"I don't look at it as pressure. This is life or death. I gotta make it. It's the only way I'll ever take them away from this struggle. My mom does for everybody else and gets nothing in return. She deserves her own house, car, or whatever else she wants. I'll die on the field to make that happen, bro."

"I never really wanted to get in your business, but I been dying to ask you about Marcus Jr.'s mother. Like, where is she?" I asked.

"Man, that's a story for another day."

I left the conversation right there and thought nothing else about the situation with him and his son's mother.

During our spring break, Marcus and I awoke every morning to the succulent aroma of eggs and bacon prepared by his mother, Ms. Baker. Ms. Baker exemplified the phrase "southern hospitality." Marcus made it clear their financial situation was not ideal, but you would've never been able to tell. Ms. Baker fed everyone who entered her home and would give her last dime to anyone in need. She was the neighborhood's mother, and after only being in South Carolina for a couple of days, she treated me like I was her own.

After breakfast each morning, we worked out like our lives depended on it. For Marcus, being home and seeing his less-than-desirable living conditions was all the inspiration he needed. And there was no secret about where my motivation came from. Together, we pushed each other for hours. Then we'd go back to Ms. Baker's for lunch and get right back to it that evening. We literally took the "break" out of "spring break."

Aside from wanting to stay in tip-top shape on our break, I also wanted to have a little fun. But, Marcus was what you'd call a homebody. He epitomized the word boring. I don't recall ever seeing him at a party, a bar, or anywhere that would scream out that he was a typical college kid. If it was anyone else, I would've thought they were protecting me from the pitfalls I faced from partying and drinking last semester. But nope, Marcus was just that boring, focused guy who wouldn't deviate from his goals just for a moment of fun.

Just to see if he'd take the bait, I challenged him, "If you were in Virginia with me for spring break, I would've at least taken you to a party or something, man."

With a serious look on his face, Marcus turned to me and said, "That might be the difference between you and me."

"What you mean by the 'difference between you and me'?" I questioned.

"I don't have time to waste. I don't have time to do things that don't lead me to my dreams. What's going to a nightclub gonna do for me right now? How am I improving by drinking Hennessey every night? Man, I'm tired of my momma being on government assistance. I'm tired of not being able to provide for my son. I'm tired of hearing about people getting shot every other day around here. So, every decision I make has to aim toward me taking my momma and son outta here. If it don't line up with that, I ain't got time for it, man. I AIN'T GOT TIME FOR IT. So, call me boring or lame because I don't do what everybody else is doing. I don't care bro, but with all honesty, you should have the same mindset."

"What're you talking about? All my decisions lead to me achieving my goals."

"Man, you don't even believe that. But, I'm not the one to cast stones, bro. I just wanted you to know where I stood on all that partying stuff."

Who was I fooling? Only myself, I suppose. I knew exactly what Marcus was talking about. I made terrible decisions, some I'd pay for a long time. But, I didn't think I had to be a lame. Many athletes partied and did far worse things but still reached the pinnacle of their sports. Take Terrell for example. He drank and partied and was about to get drafted into the NFL. I agreed I had to make better decisions but that didn't mean I couldn't have a social life.

• • •

On our last day in South Carolina, Marcus and Ms. Baker threw Marcus Jr. a Superman-themed third birthday party. Over the week, Marcus Jr. became my little buddy. So, I used the small amount of money I had to buy him a replica University of Georgia jersey featuring his dad's number, 1, with "JR" on the back.

As I handed Marcus Jr. his jersey I asked, "How old are you again?"

With icing from the cake still around his mouth, he looked up wearing a huge smile and said, "Shreee."

"Who's your favorite football player again?" I asked after a week of teaching him.

"Tootie!" Marcus Jr. screamed.

"Hold on now son," his dad interjected.

As Marcus and I packed his car to head back to Athens, I said, "Man, I'm gonna miss that lil guy. The party was a perfect way to end our first spring break. Maybe next year we can save and spend it on a beach somewhere."

"That would be dope, Toot …," Marcus began to say before being distracted by a red jeep that pulled up behind his car.

Before I could blink, a young woman jumped out the passenger side and said, "Where's my baby? I wanna wish him happy birthday."

Shaking his head as if we just lost a game on a last-second field goal, Marcus said, "So all of a sudden you wanna come around here, huh?"

"I just wanna see my baby, Marcus," the young lady responded.

"You not gonna pop up whenever you feel like it and think you can just see him for a day then disappear, Brooke."

Well, I guess I now knew who Marcus Jr.'s mother was. I walked away from their confrontation. They argued for several more minutes before she jumped back in the vehicle and pulled off without seeing Marcus Jr.

Have you ever wanted to say something to someone who was visibly annoyed and frustrated? It's an art to starting a conversation with an angry person. Anything said can set them off further. After leaving South Carolina, I could sense the annoyance from Marcus. We were halfway to Georgia and not one word had been uttered. I literally bit my tongue on multiple occasions. I couldn't hold it anymore. I turned down the music and said, "I don't know the background between you and Marcus Jr.'s mother. But I do know what it's like not to have my mother around. Yes, a dad can raise his son to be a man, but a mother's love complements it. It's some things I wish I could've gotten from my mother, is what I'm saying. So, keep that in mind when it comes to Marcus Jr."

I instantly realized the burning desire to start a heartfelt conversation with Marcus was a mistake. Because he looked at me with a dumbfounded facial expression and insisted, "I'm definitely not taking that advice. Marcus Jr. is better off without her."

"Well that conversation went exactly how I planned it," I joked before turning the music back up and nodding my head like nothing was ever said.

6

Save Me a Seat

IF YOU STAY AROUND SOMETHING LONG enough, eventually it'll start to look different. The new perspective doesn't necessarily have to be a bad thing. Perhaps, it's the experience gained from seeing how situations are handled. Or maybe it's the ability to understand people's behaviors the more you're in their presence. But, whatever the reason, our bodies can tell when something is offbeat.

For me, I peeped the start of spring football practices in a much different light compared to when we started pre-season football camp last summer. I knew the mind games the coaches were going to play before they even did it. So, it was no surprise when I was listed as the fourth running back on the depth chart to start spring practices.

The coaches could say all they wanted about my suspension, but I rushed for over 1,400 yards last season. No matter how you sliced it, 1,400 yards was 1,400 yards. And it didn't deserve being placed behind guys who'd never touched the field. I now know you can save the planet a million times, but people will always hang the one time you fail to do so over your head.

To make matters worse, they even had the audacity to place newcomer Lamar Barnes ahead of me. Although I knew it was coming, I was disappointed the coaches made that move knowing how hard I'd worked since the start of the semester. My grades had drastically improved, and I knew they'd seen me outwork each member of the team during conditioning drills. Our coaches said they'd moved on from last season, but actions spoke louder than words ever could.

It was what it was at that point, so I didn't approach the coaches to ask for any clarification on their decisions. Spring ball wasn't like the actual season. We only practiced against each other for a couple of weeks followed by a grand finale known as the "Spring Game." The Spring Game was a glorified practice played like a real game. I guess it was a chance for the coaches and fans to get a glimpse of what'll come once the season starts in the fall.

My positional coach, Coach White, must've felt that me being listed low on the depth chart was too difficult to avoid. The moment I saw him, he said, "We already know what you're capable of, Tootie. Spring ball is all about player development. It's important for the other guys to get reps so they can get better."

"I'm trying to get better too, Coach."

"Get better at leading by example."

"I can do that, just watch," I said as I walked away, ending our conversation.

Without saying it, Coach White confirmed my suspicions. Everything I did would be judged. If I showed any frustrations about my role on the team, it'd be a strike against me. Unfair or not, it wasn't about being the best player on the team as much as being a player who could be trusted.

• • •

The day we started spring practices, the local paper released an article featuring my picture. The article was titled, "UGA Football Is Back With More Questions Than Answers". Within the article was a list of questions that were expected to be answered during the handful of spring practices.

The article asked questions such as:

1. Who will replace 4-year starter Terrell Knight as the starting quarterback?
2. Can the UGA defense be just as good as last year?
3. What will the offensive line look like?
4. Can Marcus Baker be UGA's new shutdown cornerback?

As I read each question and the narrative that followed, I asked myself, *Why does this article have a picture of me?* And then BOOM, the next question hit me like a Mike Tyson uppercut. It read, "Does UGA have too many options at the running back position?" The question itself was harmless, but the narrative underneath stung. The writer predicted Lamar Barnes would be the starting running back due to his maturity and experience.

Pertaining to me, the article specifically stated, "Tootie Mayberry may be the best athlete the team has but lacks discipline and maturity. Rumor has it his suspension was due to cheating on an exam. Mayberry could benefit from sitting behind the fifth-year senior, Lamar Barnes. Barnes' maturity and leadership would rub off on the rising sophomore. Furthermore, Barnes and Mayberry may be neck and neck when it comes to talent, so going with the player you can trust off the field as well as on would benefit the team this upcoming season."

I lacked maturity because I made some mistakes? I didn't have the experience after starting over 10 games as a freshman? I knew people had a right to say what they wanted to say, I got it, I honestly did. But, the article struck a nerve. I tried calming myself down, but I couldn't. I was beyond pissed.

After reading the "lacks discipline and maturity" line over and over again, I realized I'd become filled with uncontrollable rage. My anger meter rose quicker than a person who dropped their phone face-down on concrete. What made it worse was there wasn't a single person I could talk to about how I felt. Every time I tried talking it through with someone — no matter if it was Dad, Shawn, Marcus, the coaches, or whomever — the conversation always came back to me being the creator of all my issues. It was always, "If you wouldn't have done this, that would've never happened." I knew my mistakes were the reason why I was so angry, but did everyone have to throw it in my face? They acted like I could go back and magically change some of my decisions.

I kept forgetting: as a tough ballplayer you weren't allowed to talk about your feelings. You just had to deal with it. So, I did the next best thing. I hung the article inside my locker. I'd use it as fuel. I'd make this writer and whoever else talked negatively about me eat their words. Nothing had changed in my mind. I still considered myself the best player in the world. As soon as I laced up my cleats and walked into our first spring practice, the Tootie Mayberry revenge tour officially began.

• • •

"I don't think you kids get it. Everyone has to compete for their job at all times. No matter if you're flipping burgers or out here trying to earn a starting spot," said a red-hot Coach Stuart as he addressed the team after our first spring practice. "Stand up, Tootie. Stand up, Lamar. You think Tootie is already penciled in as our starting running back, even after the year he had last year? NOPE! Lamar wants his spot. Tootie wants to keep his spot. These two are gonna give everything they have. Don't be afraid of competition. Embrace it. Competition is the only way you get better as a player. It's the only way we get better as a team. Fight for what you want every time you step out there on the field. Compete against yourself. Get better every day. Compete against your teammates. Bring the best out of them. COMPETE gosh darn it, COMPETE at everything you do!!!"

So, Coach Stuart was just gonna use us as an example like that, huh? We already knew we were competing with each other. The entire world knew about the competition. All his little motivational speech did was put us on public display in front of the team. Each person would be watching us closely now. It would be, "Oh, Lamar did this, he's the starter" or "Tootie just did this, he got it now." I just thought it was a lame tactic to get an obvious point across.

Coach Stuart's competition rant had zero effect on me, however. I was motivated by being the best, by righting my wrongs, and proving naysayers to be liars. When I took the time to digest Lamar's transfer here, I realized it shouldn't motivate me any further. I'd be doing myself a disservice by allowing Lamar to have real estate in my head. All I needed to do was be the dominant ballplayer I'd been my entire life.

With that perspective, I picked up right where I left off before my suspension. Pure domination on my part highlighted each practice we had. During the first couple of practices, I ran with our second and third team since I was listed as the fourth running back. It proved to be quite unfair to our back-up defense. It was like they were trying to catch a jet ski in a paddleboat.

You know the saying, "What's understood doesn't need to be explained?" The coaching staff didn't have to explain my rise to the top of the depth chart. The entire team understood why the move was made. But still, my appearance back on first-team offense did little to deter me from terrorizing our starting defense with dazzling and electric runs each time I touched the football.

I know what you're thinking: how was Lamar doing? The dude could straight up play. He definitely earned my respect. And from what I could tell, he earned respect from the coaches, too. Even though I'd had a spectacular spring thus far, I hadn't separated myself from Lamar just yet. He and I were now listed as 1 and 2 on the depth chart heading into the decisive spring game. Whoever had the better performance would most likely become the starting running back as we headed into the summer camp.

• • •

"Aye fellas, aye fellas, the pick is in," one of my teammates said excitedly as we gathered around the television.

"And with the first pick in this year's NFL draft, the Washington Redskins select, Quarterback Matthew Blake from the University of Texas," the NFL commissioner announced.

"Man, there's no way he's better than Terrell," I said in disappointment. "If I were the head coach, Terrell would've easily been my first pick."

"I don't know about that, Tootie," Marcus replied. "Dude from Texas had a heck of a year. And let's be honest, Terrell didn't play his best in our nationally televised games."

"You can't be serious right now?" I asked Marcus.

"Dead serious," Marcus responded. "Take the playoff game you were suspended for. What did he do at the end of the game?"

"So what, he threw a pick. You a hater Marcus."

"Just speaking facts," Marcus retorted.

"You got beat for a touchdown, Marcus. So does that not make you a primetime player?" I asked.

My comeback must've stumped Marcus. He was seemingly done with our debate. Either way, every member of our team would love to be in Terrell's shoes. As we were days away from playing in a spring game that didn't mean much to most of us, Terrell was about to get his name called by the NFL commissioner. He was about to fulfill a dream that we all coveted. He was also about to be an instant millionaire. It was the reason why we played. Not to get a degree but to be a professional ballplayer — playing the same game we'd played since we were kids but now being paid millions of dollars for it.

And just like that, several minutes later we heard the NFL commissioner say, "With the ninth pick in this year's NFL draft, the Arizona Cardinals select,

Quarterback Terrell Knight from the University of Georgia."

• • •

Whoever said the spring game was like a glorified practice had obviously never participated in one. Okay, I know those were my words, but how was I supposed to know 80,000 people would be in attendance? In the days leading up, I used every method I could to amp myself up for the game. Could you blame me? I mean, after you've battled against powerhouses like Clemson and Alabama, to play your own squad for the hundredth time would be a piece of cake. But once I saw how excited the fans were about a game in April, I was prepared to put on a show. While it wasn't quite like playing on national television it was closer to it than I could've imagined.

As the game got underway, I was shocked by how competitive it was. The same defense I torched throughout the handful of practices leading up to the spring game brought it like it was the Super Bowl. Every time I touched the ball our defense swarmed me like a pack of wild dogs. I couldn't gain an inch let alone a yard.

My frustrations reached their tipping point after our freshman quarterback, Mitchell Bradley, nearly got my head taken off. It was a simple swing play: I ran a U-shape route literally five steps opposite of the quarterback. Mitchell's job was to throw a laser, allowing me to gain an advantage before any defenders could react. Instead of throwing a laser, he threw a lob pass that floated in the air for what seemed like an eternity. By the time the ball reached my hands, a defender cleaned my clock. The defender stuck his helmet right underneath my chin causing me to fly backward — ricocheting my head off the turf.

I'd never had a concussion before, but I was sure I had one then. I thought I was back home in Virginia for a second. As I ran to the sideline shaking the cobwebs out of my head, I let off a few choice words to Mitchell.

By the time I let the last swear word leave my mouth, a hand grabbed the back of my jersey and said, "Relax, there's a professional scout here just to see you." I couldn't make out the voice, so I quickly turned around to see who it was. And to my surprise, it was Terrell. Newly drafted Arizona Cardinal, Terrell, might I add. I didn't even know he was in town, let alone here in the stadium. He must be my guardian angel. Every time I spiraled backward, he was right there to lend an encouraging word.

As I made my way back onto the field, I repeatedly slapped the side of my helmet while telling myself, *Come on Tootie! Pick this up right now. Make whoever this scout is remember your name.* I didn't know why, but talking to myself as if I were two separate people seemed to always give me an extra edge.

An extra edge was something the fans needed, too. The lack of scoring created lethargy across the stadium. Our fans didn't come to see defense. They wanted action. They wanted the scoreboard to light up like a Christmas tree.

While waiting on the field for the next play, I glanced over to our coach on the sidelines, pounding my chest to let him know I wanted the ball. After all, I was motivated by knowing there was a scout here to watch me play. I not only needed to make a big play to stay number one on our depth chart, but I wanted to create an, "Oh my gosh!" moment so the name Tootie Mayberry would be etched in the scout's mind forever.

When the signal came in, I became disappointed that our coach ignored my demands and decided to call a passing play. Our quarterback — the same freshman who set me up to get my bell rang — threw another pass that was reminiscent of a duck flying through the sky.

After the play, I caught the coach's eye and threw my hands in the air to let him know my disgust with the last play call. I followed it up again by pounding on my chest to say give me the ball. He ignored my wishes again and called another pass play that was nearly intercepted.

By that point, I'd become irate. I was that close to letting my anger get the best of me once again. But I reminded myself of the scout being in the stadium. As Coach looked at his play sheet before signaling the play, I decided to take an alternative approach. I wouldn't flare my arms or pound my chest. Whatever play he called next, I'd accept it.

When the play came in, Mitchell looked at me and said, "Well, here you go, Tootie."

I didn't have time to consider if he was being a wise guy or not. I was too busy surveying the defense and envisioning how I was about to turn this game into my personal showcase.

In spectacular Tootie fashion — I took the handoff going toward my right, detected two defenders barreling toward me, planted my right leg deep into the turf, and accelerated like a car with a turbo engine to my left up the sideline. I put a bow on top of the Christmas tree. While no other running back, including Lamar, was able to find success, I lit the scoreboard up with a 43-yard touchdown run.

After celebrating in the end zone, I jogged to the sideline, found Terrell and said, "Tell that scout to save me a seat."

7

One Step Forward, Two Steps...

THE DEFINITION OF ANXIETY IS HAVING steady feelings of worry, nervousness, and fear. For several months, I was consumed by it. From sunup to sundown, the voice of worry whispered to me constantly. It would say subtle things like, "Tootie – you're a failure" or "Why even try?" I was always worried about my performance on the field, how well I did on an exam, how people perceived me, what was being written about me, my position on the team, my relationships, and whatever else life was throwing at me.

But, for the first time in months, I felt free. Free from the things that plagued my mind since I got caught cheating on that dumb exam. Not only was I headed into the summer being listed as the starting running back this upcoming season, but I had a 3.6 grade point average.

Yeah, you heard that right. I had a 3.6 grade point average, higher than the 3.3 I had early in the spring semester. I'm not talking about A's and B's from easy courses either. My workload that semester was challenging. Along with my repeat science class and Geography of Human Rights, I also had Mathematics of Decision Making, Introductory Physics-Mechanics, and English Composition.

I knew what it was like to go through the motions and make good grades and still not learn a single thing. My 3.6 grade point average was more than a number. I actually retained and learned something in each of my classes.

In Mathematics and Decision Making, we used this math model that was supposed to help reduce problems. I never even knew you could use math to help solve problems. Using one of my projects as an example, I acted as a doctor who prescribed new drugs to patients. I conducted assessments of each drug by using data that was in large bar charts. I reviewed the recommended dosage and responses patients expected to receive after taking each drug. Using this thing called probability theory, I calculated the best drug to prescribe to my patients. At first, it was the most tedious thing I ever had to do. But then I found the solution and learned I could help people, which was as rewarding as being named the player of the year.

If I'm being honest, learning something new while achieving a high grade was one of my biggest college successes. I mean, scoring touchdowns and racking up thousands of yards would never get old. But I never had a class where there was actual fun in learning. I also never challenged myself in the classroom. I was always scared to give my all in class to potentially still receive a failing grade. For some dumb reason, I thought not trying and failing was far better than giving your all and failing. So, I always approached school with a "whatever" type of attitude. If I failed, I could always fall back on the, "Well I didn't even try that hard" logic. But, now I knew giving my all in class and succeeding was possible. I didn't know about being a doctor or anything, but I would keep it in mind after my playing career.

Aside from having a spectacular spring semester, I thought I may have a new girlfriend. I'd be lying if I said I just woke up and all of a sudden took school seriously. Brianna was a serious part of that. Her being my tutor helped tremendously. She taught me everything from how to organize my notes to new studying techniques. I knew it was early, but she appeared to be nothing less than phenomenal.

Not to compare ... Well, what the heck, there was nothing wrong with comparing Brianna to Sophia. When I think back on it, Sophia acted more like a mother than a girlfriend. I think in the back of her mind she knew how hard it was for me not having my mother around, so she felt like she had to fill that role. That's why she was always lecturing me about school and other things my mom would've been doing if she was alive. It was the, "You should go to school here", "You should study more," to "Do you know what all that candy will do to your teeth?" amongst so many other things. I thought it was the norm, but boy was I wrong.

Not saying my relationship with Sophia was awful because it wasn't. And if you know me by now, you know she holds a significant place in my heart. But, my vibe so far with Brianna was special. To sum it up, it was like being alone in a crowded room. I'm talking a couple hundred people type of crowded. You know, a live party with a DJ blasting music through the speakers sorta thing. But, being with her I would be oblivious to everything going on around me. No matter where we were, it always seemed like it was just the two of us by ourselves.

I believe when you're interested in someone, there's always that one defining moment where you're either ready to go all-in or run the opposite way. The moment I decided I was ready to go all-in with Brianna was after one of our tutoring sessions. I went on this tangent about how hard my life had become since I started college at the University of Georgia. I mean, I was letting it all out. I hid no punches. I talked about my long-distance relationship, my family, my suspension, and everything else I could think of.

In the middle of my vulnerability, Brianna stopped me by placing her hands on top of mine and said, "You should try and start seeing the beauty in things."

Beauty? I didn't know where she was going with that statement, but it captured my undivided attention. I then gently rubbed her hands to nonverbally say, "I want to hear more."

"Okay, you made mistakes, who hasn't. Have you ever thought about what your mistakes have led you to?"

"No, I never thought about it before! What do you think my mistakes led me to?"

With a beautiful smile displaying dimples on both cheeks, Brianna said, "Me."

• • •

You want to know what's beautiful about having an awesome spring semester? Turning right around two weeks later to start summer school. The school didn't require athletes to attend summer school, but the coaches "strongly encouraged" it. "Strongly encouraged" translated to football talk means your butt better be there. I don't think the coaches cared as much about the athletes going to school over the summer as much as they did about participation in the offseason workout program. Don't show up if you want and I bet there'd be animosity against you. Coaches would give the starting spot to a player who'd spent their summer at the university before they gave it to an equally talented player who decided to spend their break doing an internship in another state.

Before summer school started, I decided to spend the next two weeks in Virginia Beach. I didn't know if I was excited or dreading my return home. Anytime you're away from home for an extended period — no matter if you're away for college, military, or even in prison — everything seems different when you return. I couldn't quite put my finger on it, but it was like people were trapped. Stuck doing the same ole thing they'd been doing for years. I was unsure if that was the case for everyone but in my neighborhood it was.

My plan while at home was to stay in tip-top shape, relax, and stay as far away from any drama as I could. No drama meant refraining from contacting Sophia. The last thing I needed was a repeat of what happened at the movie theater. If anything, I was looking forward to hanging out with my pops and Shawn.

"Thanks again for the plane ticket," I told Shawn after he picked me up from the airport.

"If I got it, you got it," he responded.

As we walked from the airport toward his car, I sighed. "It feels good to be back home, bro."

"Yeah man, it feels like I haven't seen you in years," he gushed while unlocking his car from his keyless remote.

Pausing for a second, I stopped and looked around seemingly confused. I didn't remember his beat-up Toyota having a keyless remote. Shawn pressed his remote one more time, prompting me to take notice and say, "Man, hold up. When did you get a Benz?"

Laughing it off, Shawn said, "It's nothing, bro. Just something I picked up a couple weeks ago."

"Nothing, what do you mean nothing?"

I was sure I'd had a couple of undocumented concussions over the years. However, I didn't think it had limited my ability to process information. So, if I was thinking about this correctly, *Shawn — who didn't have a job the last time I was home — found work and bought a shiny, black Mercedes Benz in a matter of six months* .... I kept those thoughts to myself.

Rather than asking how he got it, I did the next best thing and asked could I drive it home. After agreeing, our conversation centered on things like the type of engine the car had to how much attention the ladies now paid to him in comparison to when he drove that two-toned, rusty Toyota Camry.

When I pulled up next to our home, Shawn turned the music down and said, "Look, man, I have to be honest. Dad didn't want us to tell you what's been going on while you were at school. He wanted you to remain focused."

"Huh, what do you mean?" I said with a clueless look on my face.

"I don't stay here anymore. And me and Dad haven't been on speaking terms for some weeks."

"Are you being serious right now?"

"Truth be told, it's been hard to find a job with that F on my record," Shawn replied.

"What? What is 'F'?"

"Come on, Tootie, felony man," Shawn answered. "It's hard to find work out here with a gun charge on my record. I worked the 9 to 5, man, and that don't suit me too well. Flipping burgers, cleaning toilets, mopping floors — man, that ain't me. I'm bigger than that, bro. And on top of that, Dad expected me to pay him a couple hundred dollars a month. I barely had enough money to eat after all that. So, I quit my last gig. Dad gave me 30 days to either find another job, or I had to leave."

Baiting Shawn to see if he'd be straight up with me, I asked, "So what have you been doing since then? You must be working for a really good company to afford a car like this."

"I'm just doing what I have to do. I gotta run though. We'll talk more, go ahead in the house."

It didn't take a rocket scientist to understand what was going on. Shawn obviously didn't want to talk about it anymore. But I had so many more questions. I couldn't understand how it even got to this point. I talked to Dad and Shawn at least once a week. Everything seemed normal — I promise it did. I told you, every time I come home it's something. Every single time.

• • •

Virginia Beach, Virginia undoubtedly made me who I am. But it was also the place that was becoming estranged. My father did little to help. When I walked into the house that day after Shawn dropped me off, Dad jumped down my throat like I committed a crime.

As soon as I took a step through the door, he screamed, "I don't ever wanna see you riding in another car with your brother!"

I thought I knew why he said it. I just needed more from him. I needed an explanation. I needed him to give me the whole story to keep me from assuming what occurred. After asking him why he told me to stay away, he simply said, "Because I said so."

"I said so" would've worked when I was 13, but not now. I repeatedly asked him what was going on with him and Shawn, but still, no details were provided. I suspected either the car was stolen, or Shawn was back to hustling. Either way, I blamed Dad for kicking him out. Even I knew it was hard for convicted felons to find a job that pays reasonably well. Putting Shawn out only increased the "do what you have to do" instincts he got while in prison. If Shawn was hustling — and from the looks of riding in a late model luxury car — I bet he was doing more than just trying to survive.

One thing was for sure: home didn't feel like home anymore. I wasn't sad about it. I suppose this was expected as I got older. Adapting to change had been the theme of my life. From the early passing of my mother to being an athlete where each game could shift at the snap of the ball, life had taught me that change was inevitable. I figured I could do one of two things – complain about things being different or manage the change by using it as inspiration.

8

A Summer I Would Never Forget

FOR MOST COLLEGE STUDENTS, THE summer was the most joyous time ever. There were no classes, which meant no studying, no exams — and even more critical — no stress, or responsibilities. There was probably a summer job or internship, but I considered that light work compared to what athletes have to endure in the hottest months of the year.

There I was back in Athens, Georgia, like I never left. The campus was a ghost town. Besides the athletes, the university staff, and a handful of others, everyone else vanished to enjoy their summer, living their best life near a pool or beach somewhere.

For the next two months, my schedule was as follows:

- 6-8 a.m. – Weightlifting/conditioning
- 8-9 a.m. – Breakfast
- 9 a.m.-12 p.m. – Summer classes
- 12-1:30 p.m. – Lunch
- 1:30-3 p.m. – Break
- 3:30-5 p.m. – Voluntary (You Better be There) team workouts

It was like I had two full-time jobs minus the paycheck. I know what you're thinking: a free education is a paycheck, right? I never understood that logic. Do you mean to tell me I had to work now to get compensated later on the day I graduate? I don't know of too many jobs where you work and get compensated years later. People think the diploma we receive is a golden ticket. I saw former players show up to our practices all the time without a job, living the same broke college student life they were living before they graduated.

I heard people like Mr. Hernandez talk about the importance of selecting and studying a major that pays well and all that. But it don't guarantee a thing. I couldn't think of anything worse than graduating and returning to Virginia Beach jobless. It would be my worst nightmare.

I could picture it — everybody in my neighborhood saying, "I thought you went to college. Why are you back here living at home with your dad?" It's like they think college is heaven. If you go to college your life will transform into a magical fairy tale. You'll never want for anything.

Ever since the incident with my brother and Dad, I'd been feeling the constant daily pressure to figure out my life. I think what stressed me out the most was not having a clear picture of what my life would look like in the next couple of years. I was going to work as hard as I could to become a first-round draft pick after my junior year. Those old sayings about, "Work hard and the results will come," better be true. I didn't have a backup plan, nor did I think I needed one. Having a backup plan was saying to yourself that your first plan wasn't going to work out. My plan had to work. It was all I had. And quite frankly it was the only thing I needed to be focusing on right then.

• • •

The only difference between me then and several months prior was I didn't hold everything in. Coach White and I touched base at least once a week. It was what he promised when we met in his office at the start of the spring semester. Over the last few days, I'd been mentally struggling with every thought of my family. So, the timing of our next meeting couldn't have been better.

Since returning to school, I hadn't talked to my brother for more than two minutes. It could've been in my head, but something seemed off. It was like he was avoiding having real conversations. Something had changed, but I couldn't pinpoint exactly what.

When I entered Coach White's office, I kicked off our meeting without any warmup. "You know Coach, I feel like I should be back home right now. Being here in the summer is cool, but I need to be in Virginia Beach."

"What! What do you mean, Tootie?"

I replied, "There's too much going on."

"Tootie, you're talking in circles right now. I need you to be more specific. What is going on?"

"Coach, I don't know. I think my family needs me to be there. My brother needs me. I think he's back to hustlin'. We all know how that turned out last time. My pops ain't tryna help him. I'm the only one who can reach him."

"I thought your brother was doing well. From what you been telling me, he was headed in the right direction," Coach said somewhat confused.

"I thought so too. But when I went home, he seemed to have turned into a dope boy overnight."

"Dang, Tootie. I'm sorry to hear that," Coach White said sympathetically. "Did I ever tell you my story?"

While shaking my head, I replied, "Nah, Coach."

"My little cousin was one of the biggest drug dealers New York City had seen at the time. I guess I was considered the smart one. You know, the one who went off to school and played sports rather than hanging with the corner boys. So, his mom would always ask me to talk some sense into him. And I tried, I spent years trying. What I've learned is that you can't save anyone who doesn't want to be saved. You can try and talk to your brother but ultimately, it's his life. It's his decision. You have to take care of your responsibilities. You can't put your life on hold trying to help someone who doesn't want it, even if it's your brother. See Tootie, fast cash is just as bad as being a drug user. The same addiction a drug user has for their drug of choice, a hustler has for getting quick and easy money. I think you being back home in that environment is not the best thing for you right now."

Even though Coach White didn't tell one lie, I still felt my brother's life was my responsibility. If I lost him again to prison or even worse by death, I'd lose my mind. So, I told Coach White straight up about how I was feeling.

"I understand what you're saying, Coach, but this is bigger than football. This is bigger than the school. I gotta go back home. I'm thinking about heading back tonight."

As soon as I said the word "tonight, "Coach White pulled out his phone to call my dad. "Mr. Mayberry, I hope all is well, sir. I have Tootie in my office, and he wants to head home tonight. I told him the safest thing is to be here focusing on school."

"Thanks for calling me, Coach. Can Tootie hear me?"

"Yes sir, I have you on speakerphone," Coach White responded.

"Okay, good. Listen to me son," Dad commanded. "You better not step a foot outside of Georgia. Do you hear me? Do you hear me?"

I didn't say a word back to Coach White or my father. I got up from my seat immediately and ran out of Coach's office, slamming his door behind me. How could he betray me like that? If that wasn't a sucker move, then I didn't know what was. Coach wanted me to meet with him regularly to talk about the things I was going through. Then when it got real, he called my pops. I'd lost all respect for him. If he ever reached out for a handshake, I'd slap his hand down. He didn't even deserve that type of respect from me anymore. At that moment, he didn't deserve for me to call him coach.

Angry didn't even begin to describe how I was feeling. I ran back to my dorm, ignoring calls from both Coach White and Dad. I was a grown man, neither Coach nor Dad could stop me from making any decision. Who cared what they thought?

As each foot struck the pavement during my run to my dorm, I could only think about packing my bags as fast as I could. When I finally entered my room, I yelled to Marcus, "Coach White trippin' bro!"

He looked up and said, "Hold on real quick." My rage failed to notice Marcus talking on the phone.

As he refocused back to his conversation, I overheard him say, "Ma, she can't continue doing that though. Listen …. Listen, I'll take care of it."

If I thought my blood was boiling from anger, then Marcus' blood looked like it was about to erupt like a volcano. The only time I saw him that upset was when he got into it with his baby mama back in South Carolina. For the most part, he was always so even-keeled. It was something I envied about him.

I could tell from his conversation with his momma that something had happened back in Charleston, South Carolina. I started to worry about Marcus. I instantly forgot why I was mad. As his conversation continued, I listened attentively to every word. I could see him get angrier by the second.

As soon as he hung up the phone, I asked, "You good, bro?"

Marcus didn't utter a word. Instead, he stood up from his bed and began swinging his fists through the air as if there was a punching bag in front of him. I thought the best thing to do was to let him have his moment. So, I waited and watched.

After tiring himself out from throwing uppercuts to an invisible opponent, Marcus looked at me and snapped, "My baby momma has lost it."

"Are you serious?" was the only thing I thought was fitting to use as a response.

"My momma talkin' about how she and her boyfriend came over the house trying to take Marcus Jr. away," he hissed while clenching his fist.

That time I didn't have a fitting response. Instead, I looked up with the most shocked face I could muster up. I knew from being there during spring break that Marcus Jr. and his momma were his world. I also learned that there was a strange dynamic between Marcus and his son's mother.

"Man, her boyfriend straight up disrespected my momma though. I'm going home right now and taking care of all of this."

"Say no more, bro. I'm coming with you!" I said.

Urgently we both began throwing our belongings in duffle bags. It was like our room was on fire and we were trying to salvage whatever we could before exiting. As we packed, I let Marcus know I had his back in whatever was needed once we arrived in South Carolina. At that moment, I felt that it was best not to bring up my situation. His dilemma was by far more urgent. I planned to have his back and once it was settled, catch a bus to Virginia.

I should've seen what was about to happen next before it actually occurred. Just as predictable as the next scene in a movie, Coach White walked down our hallway toward our room. There was no avoiding him. As soon as we stepped out of our door and headed toward the elevator, there he was walking with a full head of steam.

"Here we go," I mumbled to Marcus as we headed toward the inevitable head-on collision.

"So, you wanna try me, huh? Come on, Tootie, try me," he said in a tone that insinuated he was prepared to go down swinging before letting me leave the state.

Trying my best to de-escalate the situation, I stated, "This ain't got nothing to do with you, Coach."

That did little in calming Coach White. It probably incited him more. He began to curse at both Marcus and me before demanding we get back in the room and put our bags down. Not knowing a single thing about Marcus' situation, Coach White was just as furious with him. He thought Marcus was abetting my escape plan to Virginia.

Equally annoyed, Marcus asked, "What're you yelling at me for? I know nothing about going to Virginia. I'm going home." Marcus then turned to me and said, "If you're coming, Tootie, come on. I don't have time to waste."

Marcus grabbed his bags and left. As I grabbed mine to follow, I looked at Coach White and asserted, "He needs me, Coach. I gotta go."

Blocking the exit to the door, Coach White pushed me back and said, "I don't know what's going on with Marcus, but I do know trouble has a way of finding you. Returning home would be you looking for it. Your father thinks it's not in your best interest and I agree with him. So, grab your bags, man. You're staying at my house tonight."

"Man, how many times do I have to tell you? This is not about me. It's about Marcus." It took several pleads like that one and a quick summary of why Marcus was headed home before it finally registered. He couldn't get past the massive coincidence of Marcus and me needing to head home simultaneously.

By the time we finally got out to the dorm parking lot, Marcus was long gone. After failing to reach him on his cellphone, Coach White called our head coach, Coach Stuart, to let him know the situation.

"Don't worry about it, Tootie. Coach Stuart said he'd handle it from here."

• • •

I don't claim to be a psychic or to possess supernatural powers. But, before my brother was arrested years ago, I'd already known something terrible was about to happen. I had this deep concern for him lodged inside my heart. Nothing could shake it. For a week straight, he'd randomly pop up in my head at what I'd consider the most inopportune times. I remember thinking about him while battling a stomach virus. Who seriously thinks about someone else when trying their hardest to keep their lunch down? And then BOOM — days later he got locked up.

The same thing happened when I got caught cheating on my exam last semester. Cheating was a bad idea from the start, and I knew that! Although I tried everything within my power to cover up my tracks, I was scared of getting caught. While the weight wasn't as heavy on my heart as when thinking about Shawn, the thought of being ineligible subtly darted across my brain a couple of times. When I was called into Coach Stuart's office with my professor there, it immediately confirmed my internal suspicions of what I already knew.

The same level of uneasiness I had in those two instances was the same way I felt as I tossed and turned all night on Coach White's sofa. I wished I'd pushed past him and jumped in the car with Marcus. Something about that whole ordeal didn't sit well with me.

All night I tried calling Marcus. Each time I called, the phone wrung several times before his voicemail said: "This is Marcus Baker, leave me a message at the beep." I also sent at least 15 short text messages like, "Are you good bro?", "Did you make it to SC yet?", and "Hit me when you get this." And guess what response I got back? ABSOLUTELY NOTHING!

I hoped I was wrong about my feelings of knowing when terrible things were about to happen. I mean, I didn't know when Sophia was about to catch me cheating. Nor did I know or feel any hunch beforehand about knocking out her boyfriend in the movie theater. In fact, I thought I was going to get arrested for that incident. I guess I was no guru of the future after all. I finally convinced myself that he was back in South Carolina and tired from his travels. I also rested in knowing Coach Stuart said he'd handle it.

I woke up the next morning around 5 o'clock to avoid being awakened by Coach White. I could hear him saying, "Get up, Tootie! Nothing has changed! I expect you to attend weightlifting and class just like any other day."

I tiptoed to the bathroom to not only dodge him but to refrain from waking him up. As I got closer to the bathroom, I paused like a statue after hearing his voice. Either he was talking to himself while asleep or to someone else. I took one more giant but silent step to gain a better position to hear precisely what was being said.

I could've sworn on my right hand I heard Coach say, "So his mom hasn't heard from him either?" His question instantly prompted me to take another step closer. As I placed my foot on the ground, it caused a not-so-subtle cracking noise. My only move next was to play it off by going into the bathroom. I turned on the faucet and threw cold water on my face, hoping I was still half asleep and didn't hear what I thought I heard. Who else could he be talking about besides Marcus?

I tried calling Marcus again. Only this time it went straight to his voicemail. *I'm tired of playing games.* I willfully knocked on Coach White's bedroom door to ask had he heard anything from Marcus. He opened it and said, "I was about to ask you the same thing. Coach Stuart said his mom hasn't heard from him."

"What do you mean his mom hasn't heard from him? That's where he was headed."

"I'm not sure, Tootie. Coach Stuart said he was getting more information."

"More information? He doesn't know anything now. I should've jumped in that car with him. I can't believe you let him head home in the middle of the night by himself. If something happens to him, it's on you."

"I'm not going back and forth with your ungrateful butt! If you wouldn't have left my office like a spoiled 2-year-old, then maybe we wouldn't be in this predicament right now," a furious Coach White said. "Get dressed. I'm dropping you off on campus. Treat today like a normal business day.

Don't discuss Marcus with your teammates. And as soon as we hear something, we'll let you know."

I couldn't form a clear thought if I wanted to. Everything happened so fast. Just hours ago, we were packing our bags, and now no one, including his mother, had heard from him. The last thing I wanted to do was make matters worse, so I did as Coach White instructed and headed to my 6 a.m. weightlifting session.

It had always been easy to avoid distractions while working out. Each time the whereabouts of Marcus crossed my mind, I evaded those thoughts by pushing harder. It's difficult to conjure up detailed thoughts while using every ounce of energy in the body.

Once I got to class, it was a different story. Sitting in idleness while being bored allowed for some crazy daydreams. Rather than focusing on what the teacher had to say, I scrolled every social media account looking for clues or some activity that could lead me to Marcus. On top of not seeing one post made by him, he hadn't liked or commented on anything since two days ago.

Midway through class, I received a text from Coach White saying, "Come to Coach Stuart's office after all of your classes are over."

Forget that. I still had another class after the one I was already in. Obviously, they had something to share with me about Marcus. Why else would they want me to come to the office? I grabbed my stuff and headed for the exit right in the middle of my professor's lecture.

As I walked to the football building, I talked myself out of being worried that anything serious had happened to Marcus. I read Coach White's text multiple times, and it lacked urgency. His text lacked an emotional tone he would've had if Marcus was in trouble.

Knocking softly on Coach Stuart's door, he waved me in. As I walked in to have a seat, I noticed how red his face was. The only other times I'd seen him with a red face was after he'd been yelling at the top of his lungs to one of his players.

Before I sat down in one of the chairs in front of his desk, I asked, "Is everything, okay, Coach?"

Coach Stuart sighed. "Sit down, son. It's about Marcus."

All the air in my body vanished as I prepared for the worst.

"He was in a serious car accident last night."

I leaned forward and pounded my fist on Coach Stuart's desk while shouting, "NO, NO, NO! THAT CAN'T BE TRUE, COACH. TELL ME YOU LYIN'."

Coach Stuart ran around his desk as fast as he could to pull me in for a comforting hug. He then whispered, "I'm sorry, Tootie. I'm sorry. He is a tough son of a gun. He'll be just fine."

As we separated, Coach went on to say, "We're going to the hospital to see him. You're welcome to come along."

The time Shawn and Dad brought me back to school following my suspension was one of the quietest car rides I'd experienced until then. As I sat in the back seat while Coach White drove with Coach Stuart riding shotgun, I assumed the silence was an indication that Marcus' accident was more serious than what I was told. Now that I think about it, Coach Stuart had a knack for downplaying a situation. Say one of his players sprained their ankle and would be out for a month. He'd tell the media that the player was taking it day by day and would be back on the field soon.

We'd been riding for about 30 minutes, and I wasn't overly worried about Marcus' condition because Coach Stuart told me, "He's a tough son of a gun. He'll be just fine." But what did that mean? Is his football career over? Did he have minor bumps and bruises or maybe at worst a concussion? Or was his accident similar to the ones you saw on a busy interstate that shut down traffic for hours?

With cracking in every word, I asked, "So like how bad was Marcus' accident? Did he hit somebody? What hospital is he – ?"

Cutting me off, Coach Stuart said, "We're headed to Lexington Medical Center. It's in Columbia, South Carolina."

"Is he seriously hurt?" I asked.

"We don't know, Tootie. And enough with all the questions already."

"I only asked three questions," I smartly murmured under my breath.

I googled the hospital Marcus was in. It was almost three hours away from school and a little less than two hours from his home in Charleston. From there, I searched every news outlet to see if any accidents were reported. I found nothing.

I became mentally exhausted at that point. The past 24 hours had been a whirlwind. So much so, I fell asleep for the remainder of the car ride without realizing it until we arrived.

In my 19 years on this earth, I'd experienced the insides of a courtroom and prison, but never once had I visited anyone in a hospital. I imagined my first hospital visit to be the same as when I went to court to hear the judge give a verdict in my brother's criminal case. Just like Shawn pleaded for his life not to be taken away in court, hospital patients probably did the same but in a different way. I prayed Marcus was not begging for his life. I prayed he could walk out of the hospital without any setbacks from injuries. Our dreams were too big to let this accident derail us from what we were destined to become.

After walking into Lexington Medical Center, I was on edge after hearing the welcome desk tell Coach Stuart that Marcus was on the trauma department's third floor. I made a quick dash to the elevator and pressed the up button as many times as I could.

"Tootie, calm down," Coach White urged. "Hitting that button a million times won't make the elevator come any faster."

Too bad my brain couldn't calm down. I couldn't wait to lay eyes on Marcus and know he was okay. All I could think about was dapping him up and telling him I was sorry for not being by his side. I had to make sure we were good. We had National Championships and Super Bowls to win. I had to see my brother with my own two eyes. I had to know he would be fine.

After hearing the "ding" from the elevator indicating we'd reached the third floor, I sprinted off before either Coach White or Coach Stuart had a chance to react. Encountering the first medical staff who resembled a doctor or nurse I inquired, "Do you know where I can find Marcus Baker?"

The nurse looked at me confused and responded, "I don't know who that is. Go over to the front desk, and they should be able to help you."

After the nurse gave directions to where I could find the front desk, I took off in another full out sprint, leaving my coaches behind. Before I arrived at the front desk, I glanced over to the waiting area and noticed a familiar face talking to one of the doctors.

It was Marcus' mother, Ms. Baker. I could immediately tell the doctor was giving an update on Marcus by the concerned look on Ms. Baker's face. To not interrupt, I walked directly behind her. We both faced the doctor as he went on to say the most unforgettable words I've ever heard in my entire life.

"I'm sorry, Ms. Baker, we did everything we could possibly do. Marcus is gone."

Sophomore Year

9

I Need Help!

"COME HERE, SON. COME OVER here really quick," Coach Stuart demanded after I completed an individual drill in one of our summer practices. "Look, I know a lot has taken place over the past two months. It's been hard on all of us. But I have to be honest with you, Tootie. You haven't been yourself out here — giving piss poor effort, fumbling, missing blocks, forgetting what play is called. And if you do remember the play, you don't execute. Your teammates make a play and chest bump, high-five, or whatever else to show excitement and all you do is walk away like a sad puppy. You haven't been engaged in nothing we've been doing all summer."

"I got it, Coach. I know I've been in a slump, but I'm gonna turn this around before Saturday's game. Trust me!"

"Thing is, you don't have it and I'm worried for you," Coach Stuart responded. "Lamar is going to start the opener. I wanted you to hear it from me first."

"WHAT?" I asked.

"Don't act surprised. You've seen yourself on film. I think you're not mentally fit to play right now. What you may be going through is bigger than football. You need professional help, son."

"Like a therapist or something? Nah, I don't need all that. I'll be ready to play."

"I thought time would allow you to heal from Marcus' death — being around the guys and doing football activities. We all deal with things differently. I'm sorry for not stepping in sooner. I've watched you closely and I think this is the best thing for you right now. We play a tough Wisconsin team for the opener, but we'll be fine without you. It's a long season and right now you can help this team best by figuring out what's holding you back mentally. I mean, how else can I help you, son?"

I answered quickly. "By letting me play. I'll figure this out."

"Are you serious right now? Coach White said you haven't even mentioned Marcus. Your teammates have said the same thing. You have to heal. I have to help you heal."

"MAN, YOU AIN'T TRYING TO HELP ME. IF YOU DON'T WANT ME TO PLAY, THEN I WON'T PLAY!" I screamed.

"Tootie, calm down, son," Coach Stuart urged. "That is not what I'm saying."

"HOW YOU WANT ME TO CALM DOWN?" I screamed once more, causing the rest of the team to stop practicing and take notice. "EVERYBODY JUST MOVED ON FROM MARCUS SO EASILY. Am I the only one that's hurting, Coach? AM I THE ONLY ONE THAT IS HURTING?"

I cried for the first time since Marcus' funeral right there on the football field in front of all my teammates, coaches, training staff, and whomever else was present at practice. I couldn't hold it back any longer. Everything I had bottled within me came gushing out of my eyeballs.

I know I sound like a broken record, but Coach Stuart was right. I needed help. All I could think about was the day the doctor told Ms. Baker that Marcus was dead. When those tragic words left his mouth, Ms. Baker collapsed in my arms. From that point on everything went dark. As I replayed catching her over and over again in my head, I kept trying to remember what happened next. But I couldn't remember a thing and it'd been tearing me up inside.

I don't know what Coach Stuart or Coach White did afterward. I don't remember if I said any consoling words to Ms. Baker. I can't remember if Marcus Jr. was present or not. It was like since that moment occurred, I died too.

• • •

It's funny how fast word travels when something newsworthy takes place. When I received my suspension from last year's playoff game, I learned this firsthand. I woke up the following morning and my name was splattered all over the internet, television, and newspapers across the country. To some extent, I probably deserved it. When you cheat and get exposed for it, you have nobody to blame but yourself. But I didn't deserve what I read online the day after Coach Stuart told me I was out for the first game. There it was in big, bold, black letters: "Tootie Mayberry Is Out For Saturday's Opener For Undisclosed Reasons."

The timing of this couldn't have been worse. The guy who was to blame for not winning a national championship due to being ruled ineligible was missing the first game of the new season for undisclosed reasons. I'm no public relations guy but all this did was tarnish my character even more. I was pretty sure whoever read the article assumed I made another boneheaded mistake.

What people didn't see was me waking up every day in my dorm room and looking over at an empty bed of where my best friend slept. They didn't see the sleepless nights of tossing and turning from nightmares of being in that car with Marcus. The constant tears from thinking about the pain Ms. Baker felt. The article didn't say anything about another young kid having to grow up without a father. They didn't see the agony I was in.

Amongst all the bad things picking at my brain, there was something good that I was looking forward to: the return of the student body to campus. I'd finally get to see Brianna. After school let out for summer vacation, Brianna spent the summer studying abroad in Japan. We rarely had the opportunity to talk aside from occasional emails and Facebook messages. She did call me after hearing of Marcus' passing, but besides the obvious hurt and pain, I was able to disguise the immense toll it took on me.

As I laid eyes on all the beauty that was walking up to me, I cracked a smile for the first time in months. Brianna gave me a hug. Not just any old hug, but a tight embrace. Even if it was only for a minute, it made me feel human again. It felt good. I didn't want the feeling to end. So, to avoid having my thoughts go back into that lonely, dark place, I kept the conversation on her. I asked her every question I could think of to keep her talking until she said, "Enough about me. Are you ready to set the world on fire in your comeback game this Saturday?"

"I guess you haven't read the paper, huh?" I asked. "I'm not playing this week. Coach Stuart wants me to see a therapist."

"Why does he want you to do that? Are you okay?"

"I don't know. I mean, I do know, but it's a long story."

"I got time, Tootie. Classes don't start until tomorrow."

"I mean … I don't know where to start," I said. "I been having a hard time since Marcus passed. I haven't been able to think about anything else. I don't know if I'm stressed or depressed. Either way, I've been stinking it up at practice. If I'm being honest, all of my desire is gone."

"This is not the Tootie I know," Brianna said. "You certainly don't have to be ashamed about going to see a therapist. We have this stigma about mental health, and it needs to change. I actually admire you even more since you're willing to speak to me about all of this. I feel bad I didn't think about this before."

"But I am ashamed about all of this. I'm looking like a crazy person."

"Who cares what everyone thinks of you? As long as the people close to you understand, it should be the only thing that matters."

"That's the thing though, not even the people close to me understand," I said with frustration. "I called my dad and told him about the situation and all he said was that I needed to refocus. Like I can just snap my fingers and automatically start being the happy me again."

"And that's why you need to go, so you can get help finding the happy you again," Brianna urged with a gentle smile on her face.

• • •

It still hadn't hit me as I sat in the lobby waiting to see a therapist. *Who does this?* I'd personally never heard of anyone going to see a doctor to talk about their feelings, especially in my neighborhood. But then again, it could be the reason why so many people turned to drugs and alcohol. It was a way to push those dark thoughts to the side. Maybe if people knew there was someone who could help, they wouldn't try to figure it out on their own. But truthfully, if I had some weed right then, I would've probably smoked it. It beat having to wrestle with those demons inside of my head every ten minutes. It was just as exhausting as being in an actual fight. It also beat that indescribable vulnerable feeling I had about talking to a complete stranger about things they had no clue about. The therapist I was seconds away from meeting probably never dealt with anything hard in life. But it wouldn't stop them from trying to tell me how I should deal with all the crap that was floating around in my head.

"Mr. Michael Mayberry?" said a blonde-haired woman who looked about 40 to 45 years old. "Welcome! My name is Dr. Susan Levy. It's a pleasure to meet you."

"Hi! It's nice to meet you as well," I nervously and disappointedly replied.

"We'll go into the last office on your right. Have a seat on the blue sofa and make yourself at home."

As we walked to her office, I couldn't help but think this was about to be a waste of both of our time. How was this white lady going to help me? I was sure whatever I told her would fit every stereotype there was about black college athletes. If I said something about my suspension, she'd think I'm not smart enough to be at the university. She'd think I was only there because I was an exceptional athlete. If I told her about the incident leading up to Marcus' passing, she'd think about another young kid who had children too early. If I talked about my upbringing, she'd think everything I'd been through was because I was raised in a single-parent household. I felt like I was in a lose-lose situation.

After sitting down, I said to Dr. Levy, "I don't want to sound rude or anything, but I thought I was going to be seeing a guy therapist."

"You know, I get that a lot, Michael," Dr. Levy said without looking offended. "Besides our obvious gender and skin differences, we are more alike than we are different."

That was almost the same thing Instructor Gray said in last semester's Psychology class. But he stereotyped me the moment I introduced myself. It increasingly got worse as I hit that freshman wall. To him, I was just another minority athlete looking to skate by. So, how would Dr. Levy look past our differences and not assume cultural stereotypes based on media portrayals of African Americans?

With that in mind, I told Dr. Levy, "I can tell by all these degrees on your wall that you're very skilled at what you do. But, until you've been through the pain I experienced, it'll be hard to understand me. I can tell you my feelings or what I been through, but I don't see how you can help me heal if you haven't walked in my shoes."

"Tootie, I don't usually focus on myself, but let —"

"Tootie?" I interrupted. "How do you know my nickname?"

"I make it a priority to learn about all of my clients before our first session," Dr. Levy replied.

She has my attention now.

"I normally don't focus sessions on myself, but I want you to know a little about me. When I was 13 years old, I became a victim of sexual assault. As a result, I turned into a teenage mom. My father wasn't around and with some but not much assistance from my mother, I raised my daughter the best I could. As you can imagine, I experienced a great deal of trauma early in life. If it wasn't for the help of a therapist, I would not be talking with you now. The degrees you see stem from motivation to help others like doctors helped me. My doctors didn't go through a traumatic experience like sexual assault and teenage motherhood, but they were still able to help. Individuals who have experienced trauma often think others are placing labels on them. And some people do. But I'm not one of those individuals. I can help you, if you allow me to."

"I'm so sorry. I mean I had no idea …," I started to say before realizing there was nothing else I could say at that moment to fix the situation. I sure did a good job of judging others. There I was judging this lady based on her skin color all because I thought she was going to judge me based on mine.

Even before Dr. Levy gave me a brief snapshot of her life, I knew she was more than qualified to help me. I was too stubborn to admit it. Instead, I looked for an excuse. I wanted her to be this white, borderline-racist, judgmental, and uppity lady. It would've justified my reasoning for going back to Coach Stuart and telling him she wasn't a good fit and I was better off without a therapist. But, this lady was far from that. Shame on me for even allowing my thoughts to go there. The best thing for me to do was to shut up and let Dr. Levy do her job.

10

Slow Progress

THINK BACK TO WHEN YOU visited the zoo and saw lions. I bet they were either sleeping or pacing back and forth looking miserable or bored. How could you blame them? Strangers walking up to the cage, staring at their every move, screaming and hollering, hoping to get a reaction. I could relate. I felt like a caged lion those past couple of months. I avoided giving the expected reaction just like zoo lions often do. When people asked me how I was handling Marcus' death, I said I was good. Even though I was hurting inside. It was easier to bottle up my emotions, give a quick approval, and keep it moving. When they asked about my readiness for the upcoming season, I said, "I can't wait to ball out." That was a lie, I lost my urge to compete. It was easier to act as if I was confident than to allow anyone to know my competitive fire was dimming.

It wasn't until our home opener against the University of Wisconsin that this lion felt like he'd just been freed into the wilderness. I couldn't suit up and play. But it didn't stop me from running through our tunnel onto the field with my teammates as the sellout crowd screamed loud enough to almost cause an earthquake. I jogged behind wearing my #7 jersey, sweatpants, and a University of Georgia snapback while laterally raising both arms toward the sky to pump up the crowd even more. I felt a small piece of happiness and followed it up with a subtle smile. My smile didn't come because I was back on the field for the first time since last year's conference championship game. There was more to it than that. First, I had doubts about ever returning to that field again. Second, whether you're playing or watching from the stands, there was no better feeling than being a part of a college game day. Finally and most importantly, I had the opportunity to talk through traumatizing experiences with Dr. Levy. Experiences that were lodged inside my heart since I was a child.

It'd only been five or so sessions, but with her help, I was finally able to release the internal agony I'd been carrying around.

After reaching our sideline and grabbing a seat on the bench roughly five minutes before kickoff, I had time to reflect on a portion of the discussions I had with Dr. Levy. One of the first questions she asked was, "So, Michael, tell me about your childhood?"

I remember rubbing my head from back to front a couple of times while saying, "My mom died when I was 2 years old. After that, it was just me, my brother, and my dad. I guess I had an ordinary childhood."

Dr. Levy responded, "I noticed your posture and your demeanor completely changed after mentioning your mom, Michael. Why do you think it changed?"

"I don't know," I said before slightly pausing to gather my thoughts. "I miss her. I need her. I called my childhood ordinary, but it was everything but that. I don't really know exactly what I missed out on, but I know something was missing. Every kid in school had a mother show up to PTA meetings or graduations, and I didn't. My father would attend every one of my track meets, basketball, football, and baseball games, but somehow missed coming to school to eat lunch with me. He didn't help with art or science projects. We didn't attend book fairs or school plays together. I didn't have anyone who'd cuddle up with me when I was sick or organize my school binder like other kids' mothers did for them. I feel like cancer robbed me of a mother. It robbed me of a healthy childhood. It'll probably rob me for the rest of my life."

"Losing a loved one, especially a parent, is one of the hardest challenges anyone can face. While losing someone is a natural part of life, it does not make coping with it any easier. Your resiliency is commendable, Michael. It truly is. While it's been difficult, you persevered," Dr. Levy said. "I want to go back to something you mentioned. You said your mother's death will continue to steal from you. Why do you think that's the case?"

"I mean … I feel like if she was here now, none of the crap my family has been through would've happened. Shawn would've never gone to prison. He'd most likely have been a lawyer or engineer. He could've probably been a governor or president, who knows? But, instead, being raised by a single dad meant stuff was missed. While Dad was at work, there was no way he could keep his eyes on everything Shawn was doing after school ended. He got involved in the streets and eventually was locked up. The only difference between him and me was sports. Sports kept me busy and away from the so-called gangstas in my neighborhood. But to answer your question — I can never be happy without her. Even if I won 10 Super Bowl rings, there'll always be something missing that only she could fill. So, no matter what I achieve, the fact that she isn't here will never allow me to be truly happy. But I really want to be happy though. Does that make sense, Dr. Levy?"

"It makes a lot of sense, Michael. Think about losing a finger. Once your finger is gone it's highly unlikely a new one will grow in its place. You'd have to learn to live without it. Holding a cup or a fork would be an arduous task. It'd take much practice and patience before eating with a utensil started to feel even close to being natural. While you may never overcome the loss of your finger, there are ways you could live with the setback healthily and happily. But to do that would require intentional focus. In a very small way, overcoming death has some similarities to losing a finger. Just as you'd never overcome the loss of a finger, you'll never get over the loss of a loved one. However, you can learn to live with death while having a healthy outlook. Don't try and overcome it, Michael. Learn how to live with it." Dr. Levy stated in a rich and soft tone. "You mentioned the name Shawn, I assume he's your brother. Is he older?"

"Yes, he's my older brother."

"How close are you two?"

"Umm, we were really close growing up. I guess we had the typical big brother, little brother relationship. Wherever he was is where I wanted to be. When I got scared at night, I snuck into his room to feel safe. After Ryan, who was our neighborhood bully, pushed me on the ground and sent me home crying, Shawn made me go back outside and fight him. When Dad worked late, Shawn assumed the fatherly role. And then boom … By the time I reached 6th grade, it disappeared. There was no warning. There was nothing that prepared me. I lost my big brother to prison for the most important six years of my life. Just like there was nothing that prepared me to lose Marcus. That's been my life. I lose whoever I'm close to."

As the ceremonial fighter jets flew above the stadium and interrupted flashbacks of office visits with Dr. Levy, I refocused my attention on the game.

After seeing teammates get hype by bouncing around, pre-game stadium fireworks, and witnessing our mascot solicit fans to scream even louder, a feeling I hadn't felt in a while infused my body. Hairs on my arms started to rise. Goosebumps overtook my skin. I could feel some of the competitive juices gushing through my body like water being moved by gusting winds. The fire I thought I'd lost was back, burning a desire within me to compete. All of me wished I could strap on the cleats and pads at that moment.

Once the game kicked off, I felt as vulnerable as the time I watched our playoff game on television. Although this time around, I wasn't as defenseless as I was when I was thousands of miles away. At least by being present, I could encourage the guys. Encouragement was exactly what we needed by the time the first quarter ended. We didn't look like Georgia Bulldogs out there. We looked more like chihuahuas. We were all bark with no bite. The jumping around we did before the game evaporated as soon as we kicked the ball off. If the first quarter was any indication of our national championship aspirations, we could kiss that dream goodbye. I couldn't bear to watch our lethargy out there any longer.

Hoping to inspire some of my teammates to pick up their effort as we entered the second quarter, I slapped any player that was in close proximity on the helmet. I hoped that the slap would motivate them, but in case it didn't I added, "Come on, let's pick this up right now." I can honestly say my intentions were pure. I hadn't been around the guys as much due to my therapy sessions, but I still wanted to win more than I could breathe.

Unfortunately, Lamar took my slap to his helmet totally different than how I intended. I didn't even have a chance to say, "Come on, let's pick this up right now," before he shoved me and said, "Don't ever put your hands on me again."

We both knew he was playing like trash, so I probably should've walked away and paid his frustration no mind. But then again it wouldn't be me if I backed down. I gave Lamar a half grin before stating the obvious, "If you play like you played in the first quarter, then it may be your last week carrying the rock."

I instantly regretted those words leaving my mouth. I was sure he thought my slap on the helmet was me rubbing his bad play in his face. And to top it off, I threw in the most offensive thing I could say to another competitor. So instead of going back and forth and causing anymore commotion, I said, "My bad," before turning to walk away.

As I walked in the opposite direction of Lamar, I could hear words my mother wouldn't want me to repeat hailing from his mouth. I turned quickly to see if he was running up on me to attack but was relieved after catching a glimpse of teammates standing between him and me.

I can't win if I tried, I said to myself as I walked in the opposite direction from the rest of the team. I didn't think the blow up would cause any distractions since it was subtle and quick. But, part of me didn't understand why I always found myself in these predicaments. To dodge anymore mess the rest of the game, I forced myself to sit on the bench and not say another word to anyone.

As the game went on, I grew more and more disinterested. We were down by 14 points in the third quarter. It wasn't like their lead was out of reach. But the energy we displayed made it feel as if we were down by more. It was comparable to a boxing match. We were backed into a corner getting hit with haymakers and body blows while refusing to throw any punches of our own.

Instead of continuing to watch our putrid performance, I turned my attention to the bleachers. Me thinking we looked terrible was one thing, but if the fans' reaction looked the same, then it would confirm we were stinking the place up. As I gazed around the stadium, I couldn't help but notice the many people wearing Marcus' #1 jersey. Every memory I had of Marcus flashed through my mind like a movie playing at high speed. To slow my brain from rapidly jumping through each moment we shared, I thought back to the conversation Dr. Levy and I had about him.

"Michael, when you say the name Marcus, are you referring to Marcus Baker?" Dr. Levy asked after I told her I lose everybody I'm close to, including Marcus.

"Yes. I guess everyone has heard about his story by now, huh?"

"Marcus Baker's untimely death has and will continue to rock the campus of Georgia for a lifetime." Dr. Levy said while her lips trembled together as if she was about to cry. "Unfortunately for me, I wasn't granted the pleasure of personally meeting Marcus, but I understand he was your roommate and very close friend. What was he like?"

As my eyes started to water, I responded to Dr. Levy. "Marcus was the most determined and focused person I've ever met in my life. There were no days off with him. He had goals and worked his butt off every day to make sure his dreams would come true. That's why none of this makes any sense to me. There are people out here with no goals let alone the drive to work for them that're living with no problems, but Marcus who had the whole world in front of him dies. Nobody ever had a bad thing to say about him. I went to South Carolina over spring break and everybody was rooting for him. The mailman was rooting for him. The way his son looked at him was like he was staring at Superman ... It don't make sense. I still can't believe he's gone."

11

Long Live Marcus

THE MOMENT WE GOT THE news of Marcus' passing, I hugged Ms. Baker tightly. It was indescribable. Time stopped and my body went numb. No real thoughts came to mind. Being in total disbelief was the only memory I could recall. Nothing in the world can prepare a person, mentally or emotionally, when faced with the reality of losing a loved one. It may sound silly but the only thing remotely close to death in life is losing a ballgame. The numbness after a defeat may not be the same as when the doctor said Marcus passed away, but it was closer than anything else I'd experienced. The biggest difference between losing as a ballplayer and death was knowing there'll be another game. Death signifies the end. There are no do-overs. In sports, we mourn for a day or two and then move on by preparing for the next game.

We met the following day as a team to watch the film of the butt-kicking Wisconsin gave us. The heartbroken faces my teammates had as we prepared for our team meeting were the same sad faces displayed at Marcus' funeral. If it weren't for the tears at the funeral you wouldn't know the difference between the two. Seeing their faces confirmed my logic of losing a ballgame being the closest thing to death.

Last year when we lost our first game, Coach Stuart brought in ice cream. This year was the exact opposite. He marched straight into the meeting room, sat down in his chair closest to the projector screen, and yelled, "I swear my wife and her friends could've put up a better fight than we did last night. Pay close attention to yourselves. The film never lies. Y'all looked like a bunch of terrified wussies and the tape shows every bit of it."

For the duration of the meeting, Coach Stuart didn't have one encouraging word for anyone. He played, paused, rewound, and criticized every mistake he could find. Part of me was glad I didn't play. Sitting in a room with close to a hundred of your peers getting singled out because of a bad play was never fun. After suffering through his hour-long tirade, it was time to receive the same treatment from our positional coaches.

After dispersing to our positional meeting, Coach White went through every offensive play. Although I sat in the back of our meeting room, my vantage point was just as clear as anybody's. Lamar made mistake after mistake. But the way Coach White babied him, you would've never been able to tell he did anything wrong the entire game.

Coach White seemed to be extra passive with this dude. It was, "Lamar, I see what you were thinking here. If our lineman made the block, you would've scored."

Would've scored? Yeah, right. Lamar looked frightened all game and now Coach White sugarcoated his play. Last year, Coach White straight up let me have it. How could I forget his infamous rant in my direction? "Tootie, this was nothing but a piss poor effort. Look at yourself. You look timid, soft, and lazy. You may've been the man at your high school, but looking at this play, I don't see how. This is as bad as it gets," he said belittling me in front of my teammates during a film session last year. But all Lamar got was a boatload of excuses made on his behalf.

I sat there infuriated but reminded myself to keep it quiet. Keeping it quiet only lasted a millisecond before I almost exploded due to the double standard I witnessed. After watching a play where Lamar completely missed a blocking assignment that resulted in the near decapitation of our quarterback's head, Coach White had the audacity to say, "Lamar you initially did everything right until the very last second when your technique broke down, causing you to miss your man."

Pressing my lips tightly together, I looked at Coach White, and insisted, "Man, you can't be serious right now. If any other player did that, you would've snapped."

The temperature in the room quickly increased. It was either from the shock factor of me calling out a coach or the fire in Lamar's eyes as he stared a hole through me.

"Come again, Tootie," Coach White said after clearing his throat.

"Nothing, Coach, it's all good," I replied. "I just need a minute."

My internal explosive device was ready to detonate at any second. And before it did, I took Dr. Levy's advice and walked it off before I went crazy inside the meeting room. I roamed around the football facility until my heart stopped feeling like it was trying to jump out of my chest. After regaining my composure, I headed back toward our meeting. On the way, Coach Stuart poked his head out of his office door and said, "Come in here for a second, Tootie."

Coach Stuart slightly tilted his head to the side and asked, "How are you handling everything, son? Have your sessions with your therapist been helping?"

"Yes sir, Dr. Levy is great at what she does," I replied. "Honestly, it's been the best thing for me."

"That's good to hear," Coach Stuart said after giving me a quick, short smile. "There are two things I want to discuss with you."

I sat up in my chair and said, "I'm listening. What is it, Coach?"

"Since Marcus passed, you've been without a roommate, and I don't think that's healthy. I want you and Lamar to room together."

I dropped my head and rotated it from side to side as if I was trying to get a crook out of my neck. "I'm good, Coach. I like being by myself."

"I'm not asking. I know there's animosity between you two. I heard about the sideline incident. We're 0-1 and if we have any chance of making it back to the playoffs, you two guys need to be on one accord and lead the team together."

"So that's what it's about, huh?" I said shaking my head in disbelief. "It's not about living alone. At the end of the day, it's about wins and losses. I get it! What's the second thing you wanna discuss?"

"It's about you and this team. Secondly, I think it's time for you to rejoin us at practice. If all goes well, you can suit up this weekend."

I could've bet a million dollars that if we would've won our first game, Coach Stuart's tone would've been different. Encouragement to continue therapy for another week would've been the likely recommendation. The world is turned upside down after a loss. I wasn't complaining though. I wanted to get back out there. But, to not recognize the coincidences would've been foolish of me.

"So, let me get this right, Coach," I said while moving toward the edge of the chair. "You want me to room with Lamar and start practicing again with the team?"

"Correct," Coach Stuart answered.

"Can I negotiate the whole roommate thing?"

"NO!"

"Well at least allow me to switch my jersey number."

With a dumbfounded look on his face, Coach Stuart asked, "Why would you want to do that? Everybody knows who you are. Fans wear your #7 jersey to games."

"I want to honor Marcus by wearing his number."

• • •

"To set the record straight, I never felt threatened by your decision to transfer here from Notre Dame. I did feel disrespected though," I told Lamar after moving and unpacking my belongings in the place we now shared. "You only transfer to a place where you know you can play. You must've felt like you'd come in here and take my spot."

Lamar waved his hands dismissively before saying, "Everything ain't about you, dawg. You were the last person on my mind when I decided to transfer."

I took a small step back and said, "Yeah, right. So, not one time did you look at the roster or ask the coaches about the likelihood of starting if enrolled here?"

"I mean, I knew about you. I was aware of the phenomenal season you had your freshman year. But, as you can see, it didn't influence my decision."

"What?" I asked Lamar after hearing exactly what was said. "It doesn't make sense to me. You had an outstanding season last year. Why not enter your name in the NFL draft? Your draft stock may never get any higher. You knew the risk before coming here. There was the possibility of not winning the starting spot and never touching the field. Or, we could split carries. Either way, you left a perfect situation at Notre Dame to share the load here at best."

Lamar looked into my eyes and said, "That's the thing though, Tootie. I was projected as a sixth-round draft pick. That means I'd be fighting for a roster spot every year. I already graduated from Notre Dame with a bachelor's degree in Pre-Health. I came here to get a free master's degree in pharmacy because this school has one of the best programs in the country. I looked at it like this — go to the NFL, scratching and clawing to stay on a roster, moving from city to city, or become a pharmacist making close to the same amount of money as a sixth-round draft selection. So, like I said earlier man, the decision to come here had nothing to do with you."

"Hmm," I muttered after still not buying his story. "I hear you and all that, Lamar. But who turns down a chance of being drafted? No matter what round you're selected in? Anyway, why not stay at Notre Dame for the same free master's program? I know my suspension enticed you. The coaches probably sold you on the lack of trust they had for me. After all, I was the reason we didn't win a national championship last year. I'm sure they persuaded you on the idea of being the missing piece in a championship run."

"You want the honest truth?" Lamar declared while his body seemed to tense up. "Yeah, of course, the coaches sold me on playing ahead of you. That's what they're supposed to do. Their job is dependent on recruiting the best talent. I knew about your situation. But it didn't provide any extra motivation. This was strictly a business decision."

"What do you mean?" I asked.

"The doubt they had in you, provided me with an opportunity. The coaches felt they needed another running back. So, I used their need as leverage. All I asked of the coaches was to ensure I'd be accepted into the university's graduate pharmacy program. Plus, at Notre Dame, we'd be lucky to win six games. The decision to compete for a national championship while obtaining a master's degree was a no brainer. Even if I didn't beat you out for the starting spot, we have a shot at winning the whole thing. Even after our first loss we still have a chance. And that's all I can ask for."

"I see! You an opportunist," I announced while giving an inauthentic smile. "We lose a game in which you're partly to blame and now you wanna open up and finally say more than a few words to me. Not winning a national championship would derail your plans of being this all-academic, master's-degree-having champion. I get it. You came here to win and receive your master's degree. You wanna have options after this year. Either go into the draft or become a pharmacist. I'm not about to let you use me though …." After pausing for a second, I continued, "Now that I think about it, I bet you were behind this whole roommate thing."

Lamar gave a subtle head nod confirming my suspicions. I started to become more agitated by the second. Raising my voice, I yelled, "Yo, what's up with you? You been here for a hot minute and you already going behind my back."

"I think you're misreading this," Lamar cautioned while having a seat. "I've watched you since I arrived in the spring. Obviously, you been through more in your freshman year than I have my entire collegiate career. I'm not trying to be your best friend like Marcus was, but I do think that having more support from me and our teammates would only help. I know I should've stepped in sooner, but you know how prideful we get in the heat of a competition. A lot of the guys didn't know how to approach you after the whole car accident thing. And if I'm being real, I can admit and say this team needs you. They need the old you back. I heard stories about how cool you were to be around in the locker room. We need that back and I'm just trying to help."

"Help me?" I questioned. "How can you help me? You want me to take school as serious as you do? You want me to turn down the opportunity of being an NFL draft pick so I can get a master's degree and work in corporate America? I don't need your assistance …." With narrowed eyes, I resumed, "Aren't you from the suburbs of Rhode Island? Man, we come from two different worlds. I don't think it's much you can help me with."

Tired of the back and forth, Lamar agreed. "Yeah, man, we're different. We come from opposite walks of life. I went to private school. I've never lived or better yet seen a housing project. You're right, we don't have much in common. But we're roommates now, so we at least have to somewhat get along."

I walked to my room without saying another word and pulled out a journal given to me by Dr. Levy. She urged me to jot down my thoughts whenever I felt conflicted. Although I wasn't much of a writer, I took out a pen from my bookbag, opened the journal to the first page, and wrote, *THIS IS ABOUT TO BE ONE HECK OF A SOPHOMORE SEASON.*

12

It's Just a Game

WHO'S THE WORST ACTOR YOU'VE EVER seen? Whoever you pictured, that's me when it comes to hiding feelings. I'll be the first to admit to wearing emotions on my sleeves. What you see is generally what you get when it comes to Tootie. However, due to the chills and massive goosebumps on my arms, there was no way I could fit on sleeves to carry the millions of emotions I had. As I prepared that week to play in my first real game in months, I was consumed with distinctive memories.

Like the time Marcus woke me up from a nightmare before our first game against Clemson last year. Or the thought of running out of our tunnel with a new number on. Not just any number but a number honoring my best friend. Then there was the fear of the unknown. Would I regain the all-American form I displayed last year? What type of crowd reaction would I get? Would I resume my normal playing time or would Lamar receive most of the game action?

If there was a positive in being placed on academic probation, it'd be the hesitancy of losing focus in class like I was accustomed to doing. Although I wanted to, I couldn't afford to ignore my political science professor's lecture on public policy by thinking of Saturday's game against Mississippi State. Every time my thoughts drifted to running for multiple touchdowns, I reminded myself of the time I watched the ticker at the bottom of ESPN expose the world to my suspension.

After my professor finished his final thoughts, he proposed a question to the class. "Why do you think the government pays attention to some issues and not others?"

You would've thought he asked, "Who wants $200?" the way every hand shot up toward the ceiling. Well, every hand beside mine. I could've sworn I was a target around campus because guess who he called on?

"All these hands raised, and you pick me?" I asked my professor in the most non-confrontational way I could.

"Certainly," he replied with a subtle smirk.

"Well, since you went out of your way to hear my response. Here you go," I said intending to be somewhat confrontational this time around. "I heard everything you mentioned in your lecture about public and media attention being the start of getting the government's involvement. I think that's an easy answer. That's what people say when they're trying not to offend anyone. People have rioted and marched for certain issues for years. Whether it was about systemic racism, prison reform, fair and equal pay, or whatever the major issues were at the time. And I could be wrong, but the government only cares when it affects their paper or how they're viewed in uppity locations."

Under any other circumstance, I would've given a politically correct response. But, I knew my professor intended to embarrass me. He didn't know anything about me aside from what he'd heard or read. I bet he thought I was the stereotypical athlete:

one who was excellent on the field but dumb off of it. Little did he know, I took in every word of his lecture.

I was very much determined to stir up some mess after my response. And as I slumped down in my seat and watched the commotion brew, I knew I'd succeeded. There wasn't a student in class who wasn't trying to weigh in with their opinion after I gave mine. Rather than trying to de-escalate the small outcry, the professor dismissed the class several minutes early.

As everyone zoomed for the exit, I walked to the front of the class to confront my professor. "I didn't mean to start anything, but you asked what my beliefs were on the topic, so I gave them," I said while trying to sound remorseful, hiding any hints of deceit.

Totally unexpected, my professor smiled at me as wide as the uprights on a field goal post. "I don't know which way you're leaning on what to major in, but I think you have a future in politics. The political science program would suit you well. In all my years, I've never heard or seen anyone who has displayed a heartfelt response on a whim's notice like you just did. I don't know if you noticed or not, but you sparked conversation. Every student was eager to speak after you."

"It seemed like everyone was ready to speak before I said anything, according to the show of hands that were raised. Anyway, I'm going to give political science some consideration," I casually reassured my professor.

Following our short exchange, I walked out of the classroom arrogantly. I was upbeat after shutting my professor down. He went from trying to make an example of me to asking me to consider taking what he taught as a major. What, become a politician trying to fight for changes to our dumb laws? I reflected on his recommendation to major in political science for a second, if that. I, more importantly, switched my thoughts like a channel on a television remote to that week's football practices. My goal was to ensure everyone knew I was back to take my seat on the college football throne after our game on Saturday night.

• • •

You know the old saying, "It's just like riding a bike"? Well, whoever created it most likely didn't have ballplayers in mind. I felt great physically. My explosive first step, breakaway speed, and ability to cut on a dime were still there. Those impressive attributes didn't abandon me, unlike my capacity of staying mentally sharp. I had brain fart after brain fart. Our quarterback said the play would start on the second "go," I moved after the first one. If the play was designed to go to the right, I would mistakenly go left. If playing were a bike ride, I'd fixate on pedaling while failing to steer the handlebars correctly. Nothing felt natural.

With both arms stretched out wide, Coach White yelled, "Tootie, stop thinking so much and play!"

It's funny when coaches contradict themselves. He preached all the time how the game was 85% mental and 15% physical. Yet, he told me to stop thinking and play. Good thing it was just practice though. If it wasn't, I would've cost my team big time.

I called Dad after practice, and once we exchanged greetings, I exhaled and said, "I don't know how this game is gonna go on Saturday. If today's practice was any indication, then I won't be on the field much. It's like my brain all of a sudden weighs 300 pounds. I can't get it to move fast enough. I'm thinking entirely too much."

My pops scratched his throat while starting his sentence off with, "Umm hmm, I see." He then proceeded into his thoughts, which I already knew were about to get deep.

"You remember when we got the start time of your little league game mixed up? We got to the field about an hour late, and after seeing your team already playing, you jumped out the car, threw your helmet on your head, and ran right into the game without any type of warm-up. If I remember correctly, your team was down by 21 points before we arrived. You scored four touchdowns in one half, bringing your team back to win the game."

"It's not that easy anymore. I'm overthinking everything. I wish I could jump right in there like I did when I was 10 years old, and not hesitate and play without any worry in the world."

"Why can't you? Who says you have to worry? The game itself hasn't changed. The difference between then and now is your life experiences. You now have real problems. You didn't have to think about anything else besides playing when you were a child. You've been through and seen some things,

159

son. The game is more serious now. They write about you, fans boo you, and coaches curse you when you're not performing at your best. But at the end of the day, it's still the same game you played when you were 10. Play the game and have fun like you did when you were a youngster. Stop stressing over all the outside stuff, and more importantly, don't continue to let your mind drag you wherever it wants to take you. Take control of it, become mentally strong. You got this."

What was mind-boggling to me was to think, I was mentally stronger as a 10-year-old. If there were distractions back then, they were tuned out. Dad was right. The game was still the same. External factors had convinced me it had changed. It was the state and national rankings or the number of stars attached to your name. It was the autograph signing and the flashing lights from media camera crews. It was strangers telling me I was the best thing since sliced bread. It was your family needing you to make it so they could get up out the hood. Yeah, the game hadn't changed, it was the other stuff that placed pressure on you to be great at every moment.

• • •

It's just a game, I repeatedly echoed an hour before kickoff. But after staring at a picture of Marcus taped on my locker, I realized it was more than a game. For Marcus, it was a lifestyle, where everything centered on it. It may've been just a game when I was 10 years old, but it was what I breathed now.

My regular pre-game routine included listening to music, hoping that the artist I chose that day would get me into my zone. Before that game, I sat in isolated silence. I didn't need Jay-Z or Nipsey Hussle to get me hype. I was already there. It took some time, but I was finally in my element. Practice was one thing. I know the sayings of old, such as, "You practice how you play" and "Practice makes perfect." But when game day arrives and the stadium lights shine down, real ballers know how to flip the switch to go from an old truck to a fierce warrior like Optimus Prime. Practice couldn't teach that.

I made it a point to stand beside Coach White during the National Anthem. Once the words "home of the brave" left the singer's mouth, I looked over to him and declared, "I'm ready to rock, Coach. Get me the ball."

Coach White looked me up and down and proceeded to walk away.

"Trust me, Coach," I said with enough bass in my voice to show him I meant business.

"Trust you?" Coach White said with a scrunched-up face. "I know you been through a lot. I get that! But you've shown me little in the trust category. I can't get you to run a play correctly in practice, and now you screaming, 'Trust me'. Come on, man. Be serious."

"I am serious. Just know, I'm ready when you need me."

I'd admit, I hadn't given our coaching staff any reason to believe in me. I practiced like crap all week. I hadn't played any meaningful football since last year. But, when I did play, I looked like a future first-round draft pick. That had to count for something, and it had to be in the back of our coach's mind. If Lamar looked anything like he did last week, I had to think they'd at least give me a shot. What did they have to lose besides a ballgame that'd cost us any chance of playing for a national title this season?

I didn't have any expectations once the game got underway. If the coaches gave me a shot, I'd do my thing. If not, it'd suck, but life would go on.

Lamar started the game off well. I knew he would. We didn't talk much since becoming roommates, but I observed his movements. The way he approached the game was commendable. He studied film like a quarterback. He ate like a dietician. More notably was the way he practiced. His attention to detail was impeccable. He literally stopped the practice after a play ran incorrectly. What was usually done by our coaches, Lamar took ownership and control of the team by saying, "Nah, that play was terrible, let's rerun it." I thought Terrell was a born leader, but even he didn't have a command like Lamar had.

Although Lamar was having a strong performance, it didn't result in points. Midway through the first quarter, the score was 3 to 7 with Mississippi State leading. He was a big reason for the three points we did have. But we needed more, or we were going to get run off the field.

The most annoying thing a player could do was keep asking to enter the game. Ballplayers have learned not to beg a coach for playing time since little league. But at that point, what were my options? I made myself visible to Coach White each moment I got. When he huddled players together, I made sure I stood directly across from him so we could make eye contact. I wanted him to be aware of my presence. I wanted him to know I was locked in and ready if called upon. And guess what? It didn't work. Play after play he'd yet to say, "Okay, Tootie. Get in there."

We were down 3 to 10 to a mediocre ball club. I too wanted to take ownership of my team and take control like Lamar did the past week in practice. I told the coaches I was ready to ball. It was either their pride or stubbornness or both, but they hadn't even given me a chance. So, I said forget it and ran onto the field like I did when I was 10 years old. As I ran in, I pointed to Lamar signaling for him to come out of the game. I knew I could get kicked off the team for that, but oh well. I thought maybe they'd call a timeout and yank me right back out, but to my surprise, I didn't see any fuss from the sidelines. The only way for my plan to work out any better was to get the ball.

"SHOOT!" I snapped after hearing the next play was a pass rather than a handoff to me. Well, I could at least execute my assignment by protecting the quarterback. Who was I kidding? Instead of blocking the blitzing linebacker when the play started, I found an open spot on the field and waved my hand until our quarterback, Mitchell, threw me the ball. I pulled the ball in as tight as an old lady does her purse when walking past a group of young men who look to be up to no good. Rather than immediately darting toward the end zone, I hesitated. I was in shock from actually having the football in my hands. Then it clicked after hearing one of my teammates shout, "Go!" I took off like a rocket, not thinking about anything aside from scoring. I could hear the roar from the fans as I got closer and closer toward running in for the touchdown. With one defender standing between me and hearing, "Tootie, Tootie!" I dove toward the end zone resembling a flying Superman. The defender must've been my kryptonite because he also leaped, knocking me out of bounds one yard shy of the end zone. I was crushed. I already had my touchdown celebration planned out in my head.

I motioned to our sideline to say, "I'm back now. Let me finish what I started." My waves must've gone unnoticed. Lamar sprinted back on the field while calling my name so he could replace me. I ran over 40 yards, giving our team the spark we desperately needed. Only to have Lamar come back into the game to score a touchdown I set up. I reluctantly ran off the field. A second later I heard cannonballs explode after Lamar ran it in for six. It was supposed to be my moment. The coaches gave away my glory.

13

"Zoom & Boom"

"WHAT'S SO FUNNY?" BRIANNA ASKED after I busted out laughing from a text message I received while we ate at our favorite restaurant.

"Nothing," I responded with a slight chuckle before putting my phone away.

"Something must be funny on that lil phone of yours."

I started to sense some subtle agitation on her behalf. So, I pulled my phone back out and showed Brianna the message I received from Lamar. It was a screenshot of a newspaper article with the new nickname given to him and me from the media.

"Zoom and Boom" was what they called us after we lit up the scoreboards over the past three games.

"I see everything's working out between you guys," Brianna said along with a satisfied sigh. "But if you interrupt our date one more time, we will have a problem."

Brianna was right! My friendship with Lamar had moved on to better days. We all knew it hadn't always been the case. From the moment he walked into the meeting room several months ago as a new transfer, I knew we'd have it out for each other. I would've never guessed we'd eventually be roommates, sharing laughs through text messages. Just three weeks ago, I hated him and every member of our football team.

After Lamar's touchdown against Mississippi State — the one I hand-delivered on a silver platter — it became a pattern. The coaches were angry about me going into the game without their permission. As a consequence, I was relegated back to the bench. Not that I'm the football God or anything, but our team struggled without me. Booing from the fans started echoing across the stadium. Our coaches must've succumbed to the fans' peer pressure because a minute later, I heard, "Tootie, get in there."

Returning to the game was not only great news for me but also for my team. With me leading the charge, we moved the ball up and down the field seamlessly. But each time we were in striking distance of the end zone, Lamar replaced me. I ended the game with over 225 total yards of offense. But guess how many touchdowns I scored? None! Lamar finished the game with four touchdowns. Four touchdowns that I might as well had gift wrapped with a shiny red bow on the front and personally delivered.

After the game, I didn't allow one complaint to leave my mouth. After all, I was the one who undermined my coaches' authority. They were justified in stripping me of the chance of being the hero. But, the very next week, they did the same thing. Lamar again finished the game with four touchdowns. Again, four touchdowns that should've been mine. The team was deliberately slapping me in the face. It was the equivalent of leading a thirsty group of men to water in a 120-degree Arizona desert but being denied the opportunity to drink any of it.

The love and adoration I received last year was what Lamar received. His face appeared all over campus for the entire week. Nobody in the history of Georgia football scored eight touchdowns in a two-game span. I would've been cool with it, if it was earned. He couldn't be happy with himself knowing he was eating off of my work.

After practice one evening, I confronted Lamar. "You don't think it's crazy you're scoring all of these touchdowns after I get us into position, do you?"

"Nah! But what is crazy is we're winning," he said with a grin. "I could care less about scoring. I came here to win. Trust me. I know you've been knocking down nine bowling pins and leaving me with the last one. I may've been getting the credit, but every member of this team knows what you've been bringing to the table. And if I can be real for a minute, you're being watched to see if you're for yourself or a team player. For us to get where we think we can go, we need Tootie to play for the name on the front of the jersey rather than the name on the back."

If you know me by now, then you know what I thought of Lamar's team-first sentiments. Bunch of crap! I'd seen the blogs discussing him now being either a first- or second-round NFL draft pick. Of course, he'd seen or heard the whispers too. If me being a team player meant he got to reap the benefits, what else would he preach? Everyone has their best interests in mind. So, to think he all of a sudden cared about me was exactly what I just said, a bunch of crap.

I went into our next game with a "me against the world" attitude. On the side of my football cleats, I jotted a message to myself with a black Sharpie. It stated, "If you don't like how a situation is being played out, then change it yourself." I was determined to score each time I touched the ball. I wasn't going to continue to let Lamar get full from eating from my plate.

Then midway through the first quarter, my "me against the world" declaration was tested. After ripping off a 54-yard run for my first touchdown of the season, my entire team did the unthinkable. They bolted toward me in the end zone in a Jumanji type fashion and swarmed around me like a bunch of killer bees. It was complete madness. There we were, over 90 players going wild after a meaningless first-quarter touchdown, dancing and acting like an undisciplined football team. And if you know anything about college football, leaving the bench in that manner was prohibited. The celebration delayed the game and caused the referees to throw their penalty flags.

I learned after the game that Lamar orchestrated the celebration. He wanted to make my first touchdown of the year memorable. The 10 seconds of jubilation I experienced with my teammates, momentarily erased thoughts of the life-altering events such as my suspension, the death of my best friend, and my mental health breakdowns. Needless to say, Lamar's effort meant the world to me. For the first time in a long time, I was in the moment, enjoying it.

• • •

A day later during our day off from football-related activities, I curiously asked Lamar, "Man, how did you know to select pre-health as a major?"

"My parents were all about education growing up," Lamar answered. "I knew when I was 13 years old what I was going to study once I got to college."

"Lucky you," I enviously responded. "I'm the first one to go to college from my neighborhood, let alone my entire family. I never heard of a major until the recruiting process. I have to select one with Mr. Hernandez soon and I'm at a loss. Part of me thinks it's not as important as everyone is making it out to be. Shoot, once I enter the draft after my junior season, I won't need it. But, then again, back up plans are getting realer by the moment."

"My father told me this before my freshman year at Notre Dame. He said, the school will get every drop of blood, sweat, and tears you have. You have to make sure you get something out of it too. He meant I had to make sure I received a return from investing my mind and body in a university. The NFL is a heck of a return, but a diploma that's actually worth the paper you poop on may be more important in the long run."

"Here I am trying to figure this out in a hurry. While you were prepared for this at the age of 13," I said to Lamar.

Offering a cliché response, he replied, "Tootie, you got this, bro."

"I don't have this at all."

"Answer this, Tootie. If football ended today, what can you see yourself doing to provide for you and your future family?"

Nodding my head side to side while looking at the ground, I responded to Lamar's question. "Man, I don't even know."

Trying to decide what I wanted to be in case football didn't work out was as stressful as anything I could think of. Here we were on a national championship run and I had to decide what I wanted to study. If I could've chosen a major right then, it would've been the University of Alabama's defense.

I visited Mr. Hernandez's office and after exchanging greetings, I cut right to the chase by asking, "When do I have to let you know again about this whole major thing?"

With a quick laugh, Mr. Hernandez said, "You have three weeks, Tootie. I have to submit your major declaration to the dean of whichever program you decide on."

"Okay, cool. But why'd you laugh?" I asked.

"You walked in here like you were surprised about selecting a major. We've been discussing majors for over a year now, Tootie. I hope you've been thinking about it."

"Yes sir, Mr. Hernandez. I've been going back and forth between two really good programs. I'll have my final decision to you by the deadline," I said before rushing out of his office.

I told Mr. Hernandez a bald-faced lie. What two programs had I been going back and forth between? I couldn't even tell you what programs the university had to offer. Of course, there was the political science major. Only reason I knew of that one was because of the incident with my professor a couple of weeks back.

After walking out of Mr. Hernandez's office, I called Brianna and asked, "After getting to know me the past several months and helping me raise my grades, what can you see me doing long term if football doesn't work out?"

"What do you mean?" Brianna asked.

"I have to select a major in a couple of weeks."

"I think you can do anything you want to do."

"That's the thing, I don't know what I want to do."

"How about this, I'll head over to your place now and we can research majors together."

"Thank you so much, love," I said in my sexy tone. "You're always there when I need you."

To beat Brianna to my place, I hurried so I could at least make my bedroom somewhat presentable.

For all I knew, I had dishes and dirty laundry spread across my bedroom floor. When I reached viewing distance of the front door, I noticed Coach White standing there. *What is he doing here?* It reminded me of the time when Marcus and I saw him before trying to bolt to South Carolina.

"What's up, Coach?" I said with a perplexed look on my face.

His demeanor told me something bad had happened. I immediately started to think of all that could've gone wrong. I didn't cheat on any test. As far as I knew, I was in good standing with my teammates. What could it be?

After asking, "What's up, Coach?" it seemed as if it took an eternity for him to respond. And then, the most devastating news I'd heard since the doctor told Ms. Baker that Marcus had passed left his mouth.

He said, "Your father is in the hospital."

14

Two Up Two Down

AS A CHILD, DO YOU remember asking adults deep questions? Only to receive undetailed responses because, one, you were a child and, two, the adult assumed you couldn't handle the truth? Well, there I was at the age of 19 still receiving child-like treatment.

Other than knowing my father was in the hospital, I was clueless about the details. For all I knew, he could've gotten shot or been in a terrible car accident like Marcus.

Unfortunately for me, Coach White failed to provide any specifics of how or why my dad was taken to the hospital. How could you relay a message about someone being hospitalized and not give any background on the situation? Either he was oblivious or he was lying about what he knew. I was about to get real disrespectful toward Coach White until he showed me a ticket for a flight home that was set to depart in a couple of hours.

We were four days away from playing the eighth-ranked team in the nation, the University of Florida Gators. So much preparation went into any game let alone a game of this magnitude. For the coaches to send me home for a day to check on my father was extremely considerate. I was glad I didn't open my big mouth and curse at Coach White.

On the way to the airport, I tried calling Dad's job and the hospital. They both stated they couldn't give any details due to their policies. Those calls were between the couple of hundred times I tried reaching Shawn before being required to shut down my phone on the airplane.

I shivered uncontrollably like a naked person trapped in a major snowstorm from the fear of losing my dad. Luckily, a sweet older lady sat next to me on the flight. She could tell I was worried. So, she placed her left hand on my right hand and began to pray. I didn't even mention my father being in the hospital or anything about my family. But in her prayer, she said, "Lord, I pray that this young man has peace. Peace to know that you are in control and everything will work out according to your will. I also ask that you comfort him, whatever is going on, allow him to feel protected in your arms. And finally, Lord, I pray for healing to anyone in this young man's life who is sick or hurt. I pray they will be healed in your name."

I've never been much of a prayer, but I felt a sense of peace flow throw my body. The shivering began to ease up and I was able to make it through the rest of the flight with my anxiety in check. I gave the lady a huge hug and thanked her once the plane landed in Virginia. She told me to make sure I praised God for every big and small thing, and don't take this life for granted.

Walking through the airport terminal to ground transportation, I again called Shawn only to eventually get his voicemail. I stood outside of the airport for 10 minutes thinking about how I was going to get to the hospital before flagging down a taxi. As I approached the yellow cab, I heard a voice say, "Hop in, Tootie. I'll take you to see your dad."

It wasn't just any voice. It was a voice that at one point I was madly in love with. I snapped my head around as quickly as I could to make sure my mind wasn't playing tricks on me. And there was Sophia, sitting in her car.

The first thought that popped into my mind was to ask, "What're you doing here?"

With that trademark beautiful smile, she replied, "To pick you up. Get in."

Okay, keep it cool, Tootie. Keep it cool. With where my thoughts were after jumping into her car, I might've been the most confused person on the planet. I had so many questions. I mean, the last time I saw or talked to Sophia was when the whole movie theater incident went down. So, to be riding beside her in the car was CRAZY.

Sophia broke the awkward silence by saying, "Look, I know you're wondering why I'm here. But my mom saw your dad during her shift at the hospital being rushed in by the emergency crew. I tried reaching out to Shawn, but I never got ahold of him. I wanted to call you but thought it would've made the situation worse, so I had my mom reach out to your coaches. Mr. Mayberry will be just –"

The sound of my phone ringing interrupted Sophia. "Go ahead and answer it," she urged.

I saw it was Brianna calling so rather than make this ride more uncomfortable than it already was, I sent her to voicemail. Brianna kept calling so I answered.

"I couldn't stop worrying about you. Is everything fine with your father?" she asked.

Dropping my voice to keep Sophia from hearing, I replied to Brianna, "Yes, I think he's fine. I should be arriving at the hospital in a couple of minutes."

Hoping she didn't ask who I was riding with, Brianna said something worse at that moment. She said, "I love you, Tootie."

I froze up for a second then said, "I love you too."

I knew the exchange of our love for one another caught Sophia's attention. So, to get ahead of it, I asked, "How you and umm ole boy doing."

"I assume you're talking about Corey. Corey and I broke up a couple of months ago. But, I need to be asking how you and your new boo are doing."

Our arrival at the hospital allowed me to avoid going into further details about my and Brianna's relationship. Instead, I thanked Sophia for everything before going inside to see my father.

• • •

Less than 24 hours after arriving in Virginia, I found myself on a plane headed back to Georgia. This time around there wasn't the uncontrollable shaking. Instead, I sat as motionless as a mannequin thinking back on all that had transpired during my short time home. I didn't quite know what to make of what happened. I did know my life wasn't normal and I could probably write a book on it.

The way Coach White looked at me while saying Dad was in the hospital made me expect he only had a couple of hours to live. Thankfully, when I entered his hospital room, he was up and walking, ready to be discharged. The doctor said my father had "unrelenting exhaustion," which was a fancy way of saying he'd lacked energy and concentration over a long period. Besides being overly fatigued, it was good to know he was going to be okay. I couldn't help but think of the prayer the lady said while on the plane. I was convinced her prayer saved his life.

I asked Dad if he thought the fatigue was coming from overworking at his job. He said it wasn't and that he knew the cause of it. He said, "I never want you to worry about what's going on at home. I made it known to everyone to not reach out to you about anything happening here. You only need to be concerned with focusing on being everything you've dreamt of being. Somehow someone didn't get the memo because here you are. You should be focusing on your big game this weekend and not be worrying about me and what's going on in Virginia."

I cut him off by saying, "I get that Dad, but you're not telling me what led you to the emergency room."

"I'm about to get there if you'd be quiet and listen," Dad said in a humorless tone. "It's your brother. He's riding around in a $100,000 vehicle with not a job to his name, selling God knows what. The police are on to him. They're going to lock him up and throw away the key."

I knew Dad told me to shut up and listen, but I had to ask, "Where are you getting all this from?"

"Boy, I've worked for the city of Virginia Beach longer than you been alive. One of the officers told me he has popped up on their radar several times. It's just a matter of when not if. All that money must make him think he's invisible, he won't even return my calls. I've been worried about him. I haven't been able to sleep. That's your reason why, but after today I'm done worrying."

"What is wrong with Shawn?" I said aloud in frustration.

"You can't concern yourself with what he's doing. We all have choices to make, and he has made his. Unfortunately, he has to be willing to accept whatever consequences come his way. Now I told you this before, but I feel the need to repeat it. You can't be hanging around him and getting caught up in the mess he has going on. I know he's your brother, but you can't afford to put everything on the line for him."

Maybe that was the difference between me and my dad — I'd sacrifice my life for Shawn. I was positive he'd do the same for me. I knew it seemed like I did the opposite of what any authority figure in my life asked of me, but that wasn't the case. I did what I felt was right. The right thing to do at that moment was to try my hardest to get up with Shawn. I called him once again, and to my surprise, he answered.

"What's up, Tootie?" he greeted.

"I need to be asking you the same question. I've been trying to get in touch with you."

"Yeah, man, I know. It's been a lot going on."

"I hope that a lot is not why the police have been following you."

"What're you talking 'bout?"

"Bro, Dad told me a detective said you've popped up on their radar a couple of times."

"A detective told Dad that? Nah, nobody's watching me, my business is run tight. You keep on balling tho, bro. I'll get up with you soon."

After hanging up, I shook my head in disgust. The drug kingpin act was only good for television. How could somebody so smart be so dumb? I take back the put my life on the line stuff I was talking about earlier. I had a bad feeling it was not going to end well.

My disappointment in Shawn's decisions motivated me to start making better ones. So, I called Brianna to see if we could revisit our college major research over the phone, but she was in the library studying for a big exam she had in the morning. Acting on impulse and not thinking it through, I texted Sophia to see if she was still in town. She was preparing to head back to James Madison University so she could attend class in the morning. I should've let it go, but instead, I called her.

"Were you only in town to pick me up from the airport?"

Sophia stuttered before answering, "Yes, my mom was freaking out like your dad had a heart attack, so I skipped classes and headed down."

"Didn't know you still cared."

"I don't," Sophia said sternly. "Anyway, don't you have an early flight to catch in the morning?"

"I do. But I was hoping you could stop by before heading back. I know you're good with the whole major thing and I have to declare one in a couple of weeks. Can you help me?"

"Sure, Tootie, I can stop by for just a few but then I have to get on the road."

15

I'm Major

WHAT'S PRESSURE? IS IT HAVING the ball in your hands with less than a minute to go in a game where if you lose, national championship hopes are evaporated? Or is it seeing your family continually fight unwinnable battles against demons and not being able to do anything about it? No matter how it's defined, there are only two options when coming face to face with it. Either you rise above it, or you succumb to it.

Ever since the Florida game, I'd been on a tear. My coaches joked about sending me home more often. I accumulated at least 175 yards and two touchdowns in each of the last three games. My outstanding performance wasn't because I found my mojo. It was because I'd decided to rise above my pressure.

Seeing Dad in the hospital and learning my brother was on a collision course with prison, made each game more important. I couldn't go back home after college to work a regular 9 to 5. The only way out for me was to ball. I made it clear that I was the best player in the country. If I put in the work on the field then, I could forever live like a king. My brother wouldn't need to sell drugs, and my dad could retire. My life and my family's life had too much riding on me. I knew I was putting tremendous amounts of pressure on my shoulders. But either pressure burst pipes or made diamonds.

I walked into Mr. Hernandez's office to let him know I'd decided on a major. But, before I could say anything, he said, "Tootie, the way you've bounced back from all you've endured is nothing less than inspiring. Your mental fortitude lets me know you can accomplish anything you set your mind to."

"Thank you, Mr. Hernandez. That means the world to me," I said. "I came in here to let you know I've decided on a major."

I took notice of Mr. Hernandez's intense eye contact. It was like his eyes were staring at my mouth, anticipating what words would come next.

"For weeks now, I've been contemplating between several majors. An old friend of mine thought I should major in business economics because of my ability to think logically and critically. But, how am I supposed to keep up with that workload?"

Mr. Hernandez cleared his throat before saying, "It can certainly be manageable. It won't be easy by any means. A business econ major would involve you making some sacrifices. You'll have to be all in. The same way you're committed to football and each opponent your team faces is the same way you have to approach each assignment."

"I hear you, Mr. Hernandez, I promise I do. But do you know what I had to do? Hold on, let me rephrase that. Do you know what I had to sacrifice to have three straight 175-yard games?"

"No. Explain," he responded.

"I wake up every morning at 5 o'clock to hit the weight room. I attend three or four long classes each day. I have to be careful of what I eat between those four long classes. I spend at least two hours with the athletic trainers trying to get my body back to 100 percent. Then there's football meetings and practice. I have to watch and study film like I'm preparing for the SAT. And if I'm lucky, I may have an hour to spend with my girlfriend before I wake up and do it all over again. Now tell me, how am I going to be committed to all of those difficult economic courses?"

"I told you when you walked in here that you can do anything you put your mind to."

"I know, Mr. Hernandez," I said after letting out a deep exhale. "That's why I'm majoring in myself. You see, the way I been killing it out there, I'm going to finish this season up strong and have an even better one next year. That'll almost guarantee me a first-round draft pick. Shoot, being a first-round pick will guarantee me at least 10 million dollars. Majoring in economics, I may work for a major corporation and make 70 grand a year."

"So, what're you saying, Tootie?"

"No matter what major I decide, I'll be the first college graduate in my family. That's the goal, right?"

"It used to be the goal, but it's not anymore. It's not okay to be satisfied with being the only college graduate in the family. The goal is to study something that'll provide for you and your family for years to come."

I stood up before saying, "You proved my point, Mr. Hernandez. The purpose of this whole college thing is to make sure I can provide for my family. If I continue to do what I'm doing now, I'll be able to provide for my children's children."

"You've thought long and hard about this, huh? I'm sure there's nothing I can do to change your mind. So, if not business economics, what major are you selecting?"

"A major that'll keep me eligible and isn't too time-consuming."

• • •

My sophomore year was turning out to be everything I'd envisioned it would be. Our record stood at 12 wins and one loss. However, I didn't acknowledge the defeat. Don't you remember why? It came from the first game of the season. It was the game I didn't play because of the required therapy appointments. But since then, Lamar and I had produced one of the best backfield tandems in the history of college football. Our team was right back to the game where, for me, things started to take a turn in the wrong direction last year.

Sports analysts across the nation agreed the Southeastern Conference (SEC) was by far the toughest in the country. That was why making it to two straight conference championship games was something I didn't take lightly. Again, we were matched up against an Alabama squad in Atlanta, Georgia.

I was generally laser-focused before any game, let alone one that was nationally televised. For the most part, I tried not to pay attention to the hoopla surrounding a game of this magnitude. Our games attracted the most famous people in the world, and it was easy to get caught up in seeing a celebrity you'd watched on television as a child or the number of fans in attendance. But a little voice in my head told me to look into the bleachers to see if Brianna had arrived. And there she was standing in the crowd wearing a jersey she'd made that read "Tootie's Girl" on the back. Even that did little in distracting me. What did distract me, though, was seeing who was standing next to her.

To the left of Brianna was my dad. More surprising was seeing who was on the right side of her. It was Marcus' mother, Ms. Baker, and his son Marcus Jr. I almost broke down in tears at the sight of it all. Dad gave no indication of attending the game, so to see him there was shocking. It still wasn't as surprising as seeing Ms. Baker and Marcus Jr. Marcus Jr. was wearing the jersey I bought him for his birthday while in South Carolina during spring break.

I waved for them to come down and quickly gave hugs to everyone, starting with Marcus Jr. I saved the last hug for Brianna. I pulled her in firmly and asked, "How did you pull this off? You are amazing."

She pulled back from our hug and said, "Don't worry about that now, go out there and play the best game of your life."

I promise if I had an engagement ring, I would've proposed right there on the spot. I knew at that moment: she was a keeper. She was going to be the future Mrs. Tootie Mayberry.

As far as the game went, it was competitive from the start. Two of the best teams in the nation going at each other's heads. Whatever team came out unscathed and victorious would be the favorite to win the National Championship.

The only difference between them and us was one team had Tootie Mayberry on it. I sealed the deal with an electric 53-yard touchdown run with less than five minutes remaining. Shortly after that, we were crowned SEC back-to-back champions.

I learned I was chosen as the game's most outstanding player from surrounding media members who were waiting to conduct a live interview. As I waited for the first question to be asked, I noticed Ms. Baker and the rest of my family standing on the field out of the corner of my eye. I politely told the reporter to excuse me before approaching Ms. Baker. I couldn't imagine the millions of emotions she had. To be on the very field where her son should be celebrating had to be disheartening.

I gave her the biggest bear hug I could muster up before repeating, "This was for Marcus. This was for Marcus."

Our embrace was interrupted by the same reporter I excused myself from seconds earlier. Only this time, the cameras were rolling live when she asked, "Tootie, what does this moment mean to you after experiencing a suspension, the death of a teammate, and missing the first game of the year for an undisclosed reason?"

My body got stiff as a board, which was instantly recognized by Ms. Baker. As I took a subtle step forward, Ms. Baker squeezed my hands. It was a gesture I took as her saying, "Be nice."

Instead of coming off as agitated from the reporter's timing and choice of questioning, I took a moment to share with the national audience.

I glanced at the reporter then stared directly into the camera. "I made some mistakes and had some unfortunate incidents occur that led to a downward spiral. The media only reports it at a surface level. And I understand it. But, while it's easy to blame and call me every name under the sun, think about how words can hurt."

The reporter tried to cut me off, but I said, "Hold up, there's one more thing I'd like to say. Everything that has occurred publicly and privately affected my mental health. I'm not ashamed to talk about it and neither should any other person who struggles with the ups and downs of life. It can be the difference between feeling like you're stuck in bondage and being free. Also, Marcus Baker was more than a teammate. This is his mother standing right here. She's the strongest person I've ever met in my life. Marcus Baker's name will never be forgotten.

I believe he's the reason why this team was able to pull out a hard-fought battle today. Everything we have and will accomplish is in his memory."

16

Leadership Comes in Various Forms

IMAGINE YOUR JOB PLACED YOUR name and the reason why you were fired on a massive billboard for everyone to see. I'm sure it'd be close to if not the most embarrassing moment of your life. People who didn't know you would judge your character and make whatever assumptions they wanted.

I'll never forget seeing "Standout Georgia Bulldogs Freshman Running Back, Tootie Mayberry, Suspended For College Football Playoffs" plastered all over the news. There was nothing I could do about it. My reputation took a massive blow. The week prior, I was paraded with every accolade imaginable. But, after the news hit, all I'd done was quickly forgotten.

I was forced to watch our playoff game from Virginia, while my teammates lost a fierce battle in California. I thought my life was over. I thought I'd lost everything I'd dreamt about since I was 5 years old.

All that had happened last year made being in Glendale, Arizona, even more special. We were set to take on the University of Southern California in the College Football Playoff semi-finals. Most of my teammates were using our defeat in last year's semi-final game as motivation. Me, not so much. My motivation came from having the opportunity to make everyone who threw mud on my name eat the offensive and derogatory words they threw my way.

As the athletic trainers were taping my ankles in preparation for the game, I received a text from Brianna. It said, "Check your jacket pocket."

I pulled out a note that read, "Last year you felt like you lost everything. But remember you're a tree, Tootie. A tree loses its leaves each year only to stand taller and brighter in days to come. That day for you is today. Kick butt out there."

In my text back to Brianna, I replied, "How corny was that?" before saying, "But I needed to hear every word of it. Thank you, and I love you. I'll see you back in Athens to celebrate."

On my way to the locker room after the taping of my ankles, I overheard someone discussing the other semi-final game between the University of Oklahoma and the University of Michigan. Michigan won on a last-second field goal. The thought of competing against them in a National Championship game crossed my mind for a second. But, I quickly placed my focus on the task at hand. The last thing I wanted to do was to get ahead of myself and overlook a tough Southern California team.

The news of their win must've gotten around in our locker room too. I heard the word Michigan being bounced around like we didn't have a game about to start. Disregarding your opponent was how you'd get your butt whooped on national television. We saw it all the time. Teams who were expected to win took their opponents lightly and got smashed in the mouth. Michigan did their job, but we'd yet to do ours. For our focus to be on them and not Southern California, annoyed me to the utmost.

"YOOOO FELLAS! Everybody right here on me!" I screamed at the top of my lungs so I could address the team. "I'm glad everyone is excited about playing Michigan in the National Championship game. Oh, my bad, I forgot. We haven't made it there yet. Michigan did their job. We have to go out here and do ours. There is no Michigan if we don't go out here and play like we have something to prove. Let's lock in on the moment. Last year, I had to watch this very game on television. I've had so many nightmares since. We can't take this opportunity for granted. It's one we'll think about every day for the rest of our lives. If we don't go out here in attack mode, I promise you, there'll be a lifetime full of regret. Let's dominate from the start!"

Coach Stuart must've walked in to give his pre-game speech in the middle of mine. He removed his hat before saying, "It looks like I don't need to say anything else, Tootie covered it all. Go out there and take it one play at a time and everything else will handle itself."

I'd never addressed the team like I did, except for apologizing for my past misbehaviors. I thought my speech would've fired up the guys. At the start of the game, our minds must've still been on Michigan. The

University of Southern California was giving us one of them Cali sunshine beat downs. Their squad was better than what the film had shown.

Lamar and I couldn't get anything going. We found ourselves trailing 21-0 at halftime. That was when doubt started to creep in. The scoreboard started telling us lies. It asked if you belonged on the field. It said the other team was better and you should give up now. Not only did the scoreboard say you were losing, but the time on the clock said, "You better hurry." We had 30 minutes to erase a considerable lead. If this was a John Madden video game and we were down by 21 points, the game would automatically be over. If we were not careful, a sense of panic could start.

It went back to our ability to understand pressure. After halftime, I walked up and down the sideline letting my teammates know we were okay. Whether they believed it or not was on them, but I knew we were a game-changing play away from turning the momentum in our favor.

At the start of the second half, the University of Southern Cal's tenacious defense didn't let up. It was like looking out the window and seeing sunshine. But as soon as you took a step outside, you were met by heavy, thunderous rain and lightning. Before each play, I thought it was going to be a game-changing one. Then as the play got underway, I was quickly smothered by a gang of players in opposite color jerseys.

After being shut down the way we had, I came to our sideline and told our coaches, "It's like they have our playbook. They know which direction we're going before the play starts. Lamar and I have to be used as decoys. If not, we're going to continue to be slaughtered. It's time to take the training wheels off our freshman quarterback."

With the score at 21-3 in the third quarter, our coaches called plays that allowed Mitchell to take advantage of a defense who was solely focused on stopping Lamar and me. It was like the young fella was growing before our very eyes. He stepped up to the challenge and made precision pass after precision pass. The momentum I alluded to earlier was slowly shifting in our direction.

We fully grabbed ahold of the momentum after Mitchell's second touchdown pass. It brought the score to 21-17 with less than two minutes to go. The University of Southern Cal was to receive the ensuing kickoff. Their game plan was to run the remaining two minutes off the clock. All they needed was one first down to punch their ticket to the National Championship game. Our only hope was for our defense to stand firm and force a punt with enough time remaining to give our offense a chance to score and take the lead.

We had three timeouts to preserve as much time as possible. After two consecutive run plays by Southern Cal, that went for three and five yards respectively, we burned two of our three timeouts. The next play was going to determine our season. If Southern Cal gained a first down by gaining two yards, the game would be all but over. However, if our defense stopped them, we'd call our last timeout and have about 30 seconds for one last miracle.

All the pressure stuff I talked about earlier was off. I was wrong. This was pressure. Watching from the sidelines with no control over what was about to happen. Every member on our sideline was screaming to our defense about what to watch out for. Some guys yelling, "Watch the pass!" Others hollering, "Watch the run to the right!" I didn't know what play they were about to call. But, if I were calling the plays for them, I'd line up and try to run it down our throat. With it all on the line, you let the team who wants it the most decide the game.

Before the play started, I told myself, I'd live with the outcome. It was a tactic to keep my emotions in check. But deep in my soul, I'd be devastated if we came this far and lost. When the play started, everything became a blur. With everyone jockeying for a good view of the play, I couldn't see it unfold. It wasn't until, I heard, "They're short, we stopped them!" that I knew we still had a fighting chance. Immediately after the play, we called time out.

Coach Stuart rallied us together to prepare for the punt return. Usually, I don't return punts, because of the risk of injury, but after having a lousy game thus far, I knew this was a chance to put my signature all over it.

"Coach, let me return this one," I boldly requested knowing our coach wouldn't deny one of the best players on the team an opportunity to win him the biggest game of his career.

"You got it, Tootie," Coach replied. "Be smart, though."

As I lined up for the return, I knew there was no way the punter was dumb enough to kick it to me.

After locating the ball in the air, I quickly scanned the field to see if there was enough room for a return. *He is that dumb.* There were no more thoughts aside from ensuring I caught the ball and turning into a complete savage afterward.

I found a gap in the defense and ran as fast as I could through it. The crowd got louder and louder the further I ran. It was a sign: I was doing the impossible. I became over-anxious once the end zone was in sight. I thought I had just enough in my tank to outrun the last defender, but I was on empty. The defender tripped me up at the five-yard line with fifteen-seconds remaining.

We had time for maybe two chances at a game-winning play. Mitchell huddled us up and called a play that was intended for me.

As bad as I wanted to play hero, I told him, "You have to change the play when we line up. They're expecting me to get it."

Like a seasoned quarterback, he audibled the play at the line. He shifted both, Lamar and me out of the backfield in opposite directions. After quickly snapping the ball, he faked a pass to me, which drew the attention of most the Southern Cal defenders. Then, he shifted his head in Lamar's direction and threw a bullet to him for the game-winning touchdown. The legend of Mitchell Bradley was born. Seconds later, we were Fiesta Bowl champions and national championship bound.

Immediately after the game, a pumped-up Coach White found me and said, "The stat sheet doesn't show the leadership you displayed tonight, Tootie. It was all about the team. We don't pull this one out without your leadership. I'm proud of you."

"Thank you, Coach. There's something I meant to tell you," I said while extending my hand for a handshake. "Who knows, if I'd gotten into the car with Marcus what would've happened. I like to think if I was there, he would've never gotten into a car accident. But, it could've been both of us who died that night. I want to say sorry. The way I've been acting toward you since that night has been unacceptable. Thank you for saving my life."

Our heart-to-heart was interrupted by teammates who were turnt up and celebrating our victory. I jumped around with joy for a couple of minutes before finding a quiet place to reflect. These were the moments that made going through bad situations worth it. We had a chance to win our first national championship in decades. Other than making it to the NFL, winning a title was the reason I chose Georgia — and having the chance to do it my sophomore year was more than I could ask for.

When I went into the locker room, I called Brianna to thank her for supporting me along the way. I also said, "I know I didn't play my best game, but it feels good to be heading to the ship."

Brianna replied, "What do you mean, you didn't play your best? If it wasn't for your punt return, we would've lost. Anyway, my flight is booked for the championship game. I can't wait to see you tomorrow so we can have our own celebration."

• • •

The next day we arrived in Georgia to a massive celebratory crowd waiting at the airport. The scene was reminiscent of an inauguration for a newly elected President of the United States. I couldn't imagine what it'd be like after we were crowned champions in a week. Coach Stuart made it clear: he wanted us to shake hands with as many people as we could for at least an hour. I participated in the fake love because I was required to do so. These fans didn't care about me as a person. To them, I was just a commodity, they only cared about me on the field. Although I didn't like it, I understood it better than I did last year. Even being a student-athlete was a business. I gave as many high-fives, autographs, and inauthentic smiles as I could. I couldn't wait to be with my real fan. I was eager to see what Brianna had planned for our celebration.

I asked Lamar if he could drop me off at Brianna's apartment once we arrived at his car after we departed the airport. On the way to Brianna's place, Lamar turned down his music to say, "Man, I scored the game-winning touchdown of a major Bowl game to send us to the championship. You don't know how crazy that was for me."

"It was big-time, bro," I chimed in.

"I got to thinking last night about you telling Mitchell to change the play in the huddle. That's not the Tootie I've gotten to know. Man, be real, you wanted me to score that touchdown."

"What? What're you talkin' about?" I asked.

"You know what I'm talkin' about."

"Aight, bro. This is what you came here for. I didn't know for sure Mitchell was going to find you in the end zone the way he did, but I hoped it was you."

Lamar started saying something else as we pulled in front of Brianna's apartment, but I tuned him out due to being distracted by my phone ringing. I decided not to answer it so I could ask Lamar to repeat what he was saying.

"I said, I can't thank –," he started to say before I interrupted him.

I told Lamar, "My bad, bro. Back home is calling me. It might be about my dad again. Hold that thought."

It was Sophia calling for the second straight time. All I could think about was my dad being hospitalized again, so this time I answered.

After saying hello, Sophia said, "You remember the night you asked me to come over to talk about what you wanted to major in?"

"Yes, I remember," I answered.

"We should've kept our conversation to just that."

"What do you mean, Sophia?"

"I'm pregnant. I'm pregnant. My life is over, Tootie. What am I supposed to do now?"

Coming Soon...

THE ATHLETE-STUDENT:
Junior Year

Acknowledgments

I have been so overwhelmed by the support and connections I've made since the release of 'Freshman Year.' While I have higher aspirations for the book series, I couldn't have predicted how quickly everything has come together. It all starts with my faith in God. There have been many times I've experienced doubts, anxiety, and frustration to only be inspired to keep pushing through because of my relationship with Christ.

To my wife, thank you for your patience. Finishing up my last year before becoming Dr. Holloman, work, and writing this novel has been no easy feat. But, your encouragement has helped me to keep going.

To my three foster children – the Three T's. I love you as if you were my biological children. I have no idea where life will lead us, but thank you for showing me how to love. I pray for you every day and have faith; you all will be just fine.

Special thanks to a group of great men – Moe Holloman, Shawn Baxter, Don Carey, Travis "Trigga" Stevens, Ike Madison, Corey Parrish, Andrew Curtis, Keith Madison, Brad Holloman, Whodi Wright, Mitchell Faulkner, Dr. Bobby White,

Aaron Ransom, Josh Anderson, Corey Davis, Shelton Johnson, James Callaham, Antoine Henderson, Dominque White & Deltonio Thompson. You guys have listened and given me countless advice throughout this book-writing journey. Thank you all so much for your support and encouragement these past 12 months.

To my parents, Aunt Von, Aunt Jensie, Momma Jackson, Mr. Jackson, Uncle Man, Aunt Nee, Tamieca Holloman, Dangelo Fletcher, and the rest of my family, thank you for everything you do. Last and not least: thank you to everyone who has purchased, read, and shared the novel. #Keeppushing.

In loving memory to my uncle Antoine Holloman.

THE ATHLETE-STUDENT:

Sophomore Year

www.ingramcontent.com/pod-product-compliance
Lightning Source LLC
Chambersburg PA
CBHW022142240626
47153CB00007B/2465